SHADOWS OVER
BIGELOW MANOR

D1606317

SHADOWS OVER BIGELOW MANOR

Judy Conlin

Authors Choice Press

New York Lincoln Shanghai

Shadows Over Bigelow Manor

Authors Choice Press
an imprint of iUniverse, Inc.

iUniverse books may be ordered through booksellers or by contacting:

iUniverse
2021 Pine Lake Road, Suite 100
Lincoln, NE 68512
www.iuniverse.com
1-800-Authors (1-800-288-4677)

Originally published by Avalon Books

Originally published as Nurse Julie's Image

This is a work of fiction. All of the characters, names, incidents, organizations, and dialogue in this novel are either the products of the author's imagination or are used fictitiously.

ISBN: 978-0-595-45359-7

Printed in the United States of America

SHADOWS OVER BIGELOW MANOR

CHAPTER ONE

"Julie, stop packing and listen to me." Doreen looked uneasily at her younger sister, who was closing one of her suitcases. "There's no need for you to take this job. If you don't want to return to the hospital, there are plenty of other opportunities for nurses right here around Norson, and you can continue staying with Mark and me."

Julie smiled at Doreen affectionately, then turned her attention to another suitcase that was almost full. She glanced around the tiny spare room. "Newlyweds like you two need privacy, not company. And I've already been here six weeks."

For a moment their eyes misted and words faltered as both girls were reminded of the reason for Julie's being

1

there at all—the boating accident that had taken their parents' lives.

After using what little insurance money there was to bury them, Julie and Doreen had sold the family furnishings in the rented Jacobs home. Then Julie had moved in with her only sister, recently married to Mark Cullen.

Grief had kept Julie numb for several weeks, and she continued her hospital nursing job in something like a state of shock. But eventually she realized she must find a new job and a new life somewhere else, away from the heartbreaking memories. Besides, a part of her had always wanted to move away from Norson, and this seemed like the right time. So she'd answered an ad in a nursing journal.

"Wanted," it had read, "nurse companion for elderly woman. Live-in position. Plain type with few family ties preferred. Completely answerable to male head of household. Ability to follow orders implicitly and keep to self in free time more important than wide nursing experience. Luxurious accommodations in fine old mansion near park. Easy access to large

metropolitan area. Good pay. Send resume and recent photo with your reply."
Then the box number was given.

A strange ad, Julie thought. Almost a
little scary. But she was attracted to the
offer of good pay and the idea of living in
a mansion near a large metropolitan
area. So she sent a letter to the indicated
box number with her resume and the
plainest picture of herself she could find.
To her surprise, she received a letter of
acceptance by return mail. Next there
were some phone calls, and a starting
date for the new job was agreed upon.
Once that was done, Julie gave notice at
the Norson County Hospital where she
had worked for the past eighteen
months.

Now Julie smiled and turned her ex-
pressive dark eyes, which didn't look
plain at all, toward her sister. "This is
my big adventure, Doreen. You know I've
never been more than twenty-five miles
from home in my entire twenty-two
years. It's time I saw a little of the world.
Besides, I'll still be in New York State."

Doreen hugged her but looked a little
doubtful, for Julie had always been on

the timid side. "I just want you to be happy in Buffalo, honey."

"I know that, and I will be," Julie declared, hoping she was speaking the truth. The thought of going off on her own both fascinated and frightened her. She couldn't get the unusual wording of the ad out of her mind. But she felt she had to take that job.

"How are my two best girls?" Julie's brother-in-law asked from the doorway.

Looking up, Julie said, "Mark, you're just in time. Tell Doreen she mustn't begrudge a poor spinster sister an exciting adventure just because she's an old married woman now."

While everyone laughed, Julie finished her packing. Soon the bags were carried down to the front porch and Julie quickly showered and put on her traveling clothes: a neat blue suit and white blouse. Then she, Doreen, and Mark walked outside.

Before the assembled trio had time to reflect on the imminent parting, Jim Wick drove up in his battered green car to take Julie to the train station ten miles away. As he unwound himself from behind the steering wheel, Julie was truly happy about leaving for the first time. Dear, devoted Jim had been her constant pursuer since their high-school days. As he peered at her now through his thick wire-rimmed glasses, she saw his warm brown eyes light up in answer to her smile.

"Ready, hon?" he asked.

She nodded affectionately, knowing how much he wanted her to stay in Norson. If she stayed here, she realized someday she'd probably marry him, raise a houseful of kids, and never know what might have been. Yet her parents' unexpected death, in addition to being a great loss, had reminded her that all life was finite. And if she wanted to see more of the world, meet more people, she knew she should start. Very soon. Now she was on the verge of doing exactly that.

"You know you have a home here any time you want it," Mark said as Julie turned and gave him a quick hug.

Doreen embraced her tearfully. "Write. Don't forget to write."

"Of course I won't," Julie said.

Turning away quickly to hide her face,

Doreen grabbed a yellow-and-blue-plaid valise. Mark took the two bigger ones, and soon they were all in the trunk of the little green car.

It wasn't long before Julie was on the train to Buffalo.

"Where to, lady?" the Buffalo cab-driver asked once Julie and her luggage were safely installed in his taxi.

Fumbling through her handbag, she extracted a piece of paper with the needed information and spent the rest of the trip trying to block out her final image of Jim. He'd looked so sad at the train station. No longer did he seem dull. Instead, he represented stability, security, and all the good things Julie had left behind.

With no interest in the passing scene, she found herself thinking about that want ad once more. Why should someone ask for a photograph when hiring a nurse, and why should they want one with few family ties, one who was willing to obey orders unquestioningly?

Above all, why had she kept the details of that ad from Doreen, Mark, and

Jim? She could be walking into some kind of weird situation. She might need help.

Well, for once she would just have to handle things on her own. Somehow Julie dismissed her sudden fears and lifted her small, dimpled chin in a surprisingly determined fashion.

CHAPTER TWO

Julie felt very vulnerable after the cabdriver dropped her and her luggage off at the designated address on the outskirts of Buffalo.

Her feeling of helplessness intensified as she gazed around her. She was standing on a sidewalk across the street from a huge park. In front of her was a high iron fence, and off to the far left and the far right were beautifully manicured lawns with huge mansions set far back from the street. But Julie could not yet see the house that belonged to her new employer.

Nervously straightening her skirt, she turned her attention to the big, handsomely ornamented wrought-iron gates in the fence before her, gates with the initial B worked into their scrollwork. A tentative push revealed the gates were

8

locked, and for a moment Julie was at a loss as to what she should do next. After all, if she couldn't even see the house, it seemed unlikely that anyone at the house could see her. Then she suddenly noticed a small button like a doorbell.

When she pushed it, an electronic voice immediately said, "What is your business?"

"I'm Julie Jacobs, and I'm Mrs. Bigelow's new nurse companion."

Almost immediately the big gates began to slide apart with a kind of electrical whir. Julie moved her luggage and herself through as fast as she could, for she had no idea how long the gates would remain open. As it happened, they clanged shut right behind her.

A harsh laugh was heard as Julie hopped around to retrieve a shoe she'd somehow lost in her hurry. Angrily she tried to regain dignity. Then she discovered where the laugh came from: a small gatehouse cleverly hidden in the greenery so it couldn't be seen from the sidewalk. The sole occupant, high up in the tower-like structure, was holding a microphone and shaking with mirth.

Julie's cheeks burned as she glared at the insolent red-haired young man now making his way down from the tower. Impulsively she turned her back on him and stalked off in what she hoped was the direction of the house.

"To your right, Miss High and Mighty. To your right."

Hearing his sarcastic instructions, Julie veered to the right but otherwise ignored him.

The Bigelow mansion wasn't very far from the gates. It was just heavily camouflaged with trees. As Julie stepped closer, she saw it was a vast, dark Victorian structure perched on a knoll like a large bird clutching its prey. At the moment fat gray clouds hung above it, adding to the gloom.

Wide steps led up to a big porch adorned by gingerbread. Four stories high, the house had rounded turrets at each end. It showed few other signs of symmetry. The windows were of various sizes and shapes, some of them quite unusual. Julie's eyes went from one window to the next in fascination, until her attention was riveted by a slight movement behind a pagoda-like window on the third floor. Was someone there? she asked herself.

Her thoughts were interrupted by the red-haired young man.

"Figured you might be needing these," he said, putting down the luggage, which she'd left near the gate.

Julie hesitated. Old habits were hard to break. Should she thank him? Or should she let him know she resented his attitude?

She stuck out her chin. "I planned to send for my things."

"Forgive me, your ladyship." His lips became a thin line in his square freckled face. "I suppose you'll call a footman?"

"I really don't want to discuss this with a—a—a gateman," Julie stammered, feeling very inadequate.

"No need to, ma'am. I'll be on my way." And with a mock bow, he turned on his heel.

Julie watched his departure, trying to control the trembling in her hands. Her cheeks were flushed, but whether from anger or embarrassment she wasn't sure. She noticed his muscles under his T-shirt. There was no denying he was quite attractive... and quite arrogant, she admitted to herself.

Just as she was about to turn away, he twisted his neck around toward her. A startled expression darted across his face.

"The other one was exactly the same," he called over his shoulder. "The spitting image. Pretty as a picture, but real nasty inside. He sure does have a knack for finding 'em."

Julie stared at him. What was the man talking about? Had another nurse been lured to this place recently? If so, what had happened to her? Was something strange going on in this big dark house? A little shiver ran down her spine.

Then, shrugging her shoulders as if to dismiss such thoughts, she picked up her luggage and started up the porch.

CHAPTER THREE

A short time after Julie rang the bell, the front door slowly began to open. It all seemed so eerie. A tall, gaunt gray-haired woman—doubtlessly a house-keeper—was revealed in the widening gap. Gray suede shoes and a gray uniform made her all one color from head to foot. And she seemed to emit a scent of mothballs.

As she glanced at Julie's face, a startled look came into her gray eyes. "What is it you want?"

"My name is Julie Jacobs. Mr. Bigelow is expecting me," she managed in what she hoped was a firm voice.

"I'll check with him." The gray figure silently whirled out of sight, leaving Julie alone.

Having nothing else to do, she inspected the entry hall. It had a high-domed ceiling with an antique Tiffany lamp, which gave out a muted light. Long strings of beads hanging from the edges glittered coldly.

Nearby were several pieces of antique furniture, including two high-backed chairs with maroon velvet seats, flanking an ornate full-length mirror. Julie slowly walked over to the mirror to stare at her pale face and untidy dark hair. As her hands automatically pushed some unruly locks behind her ears, she saw a sudden movement behind her that made her spin around nervously.

A plump blond figure with a feather duster appeared even more startled than Julie. "Ahh!" she shrieked, her fat little fingers clamped over her rose-red mouth. The feather duster clattered to the floor and the girl ran into some room as if a demon were nipping at her heels.

"What's the matter?" Julie called after her. "Is anything wrong?"

She stepped over the feather duster, stifling a sudden impulse to giggle as she imagined the round little maid flying up to the Tiffany lamp like a chubby cherub in order to dust it.

Curiosity made Julie step through the door the maid had just taken only to find herself alone in a huge library.

"There must be thousands of books here," she murmured as she looked at the shelves covering most of the four walls. She couldn't help thinking of her few boxes of books now kept in her sister's attic because of a lack of space.

Examining the shelves, Julie saw all kinds of old and new books: novels, biographies, plays, reference books, poetry, science fiction, everything.

They've got to let me use this library, she told herself, for she was an avid reader.

Julie had begun to look through a book of poems when she heard a noise behind her. As she turned her head to see what had caused it, two figures scuttled away quickly, but not before she recognized her plump feather-duster friend with a mousy companion, who wore the same startled expression Julie had been seeing since arriving.

They must all be crazy, she thought, putting the book away and walking to the doorway.

Just then the unfriendly woman in gray approached and told Julie, "He says he'll see you. Follow me."

Julie noticed the gray eyes were focused on a spot above her head. She followed that gaze to a large portrait over the fireplace, which she'd surely have noticed before if she hadn't been so engrossed in looking at the book titles.

The portrait stunned Julie. She looked at the housekeeper for an explanation. The woman's thin lips twisted upward in a faint mocking smile. But she said nothing. She merely turned around and reentered the hall. Julie hurried after her, her head full of questions, the main one being: How in the world did a painting that looked just like Julie come to be hanging in the library of Bigelow Manor?

CHAPTER FOUR

The small study Julie now entered seemed monastic. The walls were white and bare. And the furniture was sparse. A massive desk and swivel chair stood in the center of the room. There were two straight-backed chairs nearby.

In the swivel chair sat the handsomest man Julie had ever seen. He seemed to be in his middle thirties and had very dark hair, black eyes, and prominent cheekbones.

Julie recognized his voice from their telephone conversations when he harshly told the housekeeper, "That will be all, Mrs. Fynn." He turned to Julie as the gray specter vanished. "You, then, are Miss Jacobs."

"Julie, if you please, sir," she murmured, wishing he didn't look so un-

17

friendly in his immaculate, well-pressed clothes. "I want to be called Julie."

His cold dark eyes fastened on her almost with distaste. "I shall call you Miss Jacobs," he said. "How the other members of the household wish to address you is of no consequence to me. Your duties here concern my mother. She's not really ill, although she is taking medication for her blood pressure. She also suffers from arthritis and various other minor maladies associated with her age. Mainly, however, she suffers from boredom. Your job, Miss Jacobs, is to relieve that boredom. Do you understand?"

Julie nodded with sinking spirits. Her medical training was to be wasted on entertaining a spoiled rich woman. This wasn't at all how she'd envisioned her great adventure.

"Mother can seem a little difficult at times, but that's only because she's bored. If you do your job adequately, there should be no problem."

Julie groaned inwardly. Naturally, with his attitude, if any "problems" arose, he would blame them on her.

"You will have one day off a week when the maids will look after Mother. What you do with this day, of course, is up to you. But under no circumstances are you to expect me to become involved with entertaining you. The various Bigelow holdings—which include real estate, office buildings, and other things—require a substantial amount of my time. I'll have no time to devote to you that does not relate directly to your employment. And other than your day off, your time belongs mostly to your patient. She will let you know the hours she needs you, when she wishes to rest, and so on. You are to follow her wishes in all things. You'll have your own room and take your meals with the family. Payday will be the first day of the month. Do you have any questions?"

Julie's head was reeling. If the mother was anything like her son, she would be a very difficult patient. Still, Julie had taken care of all types before and she was sure she could manage.

"Who does the family consist of?" she asked.

"If you mean who you'll be eating with

in the dining room, there's my mother, my cousin, myself, and whatever guests we might have."

Julie was annoyed that he'd read her thoughts so accurately. She was also surprised that such a handsome man was unmarried. Of course, who would want to marry such an arrogant stiff? she asked herself.

"Your cousin?" She left a question mark in her voice.

"Yes, Daniel Bigelow. He's staying with us while he attends school. You'll meet him tonight!" He stood up impatiently, and Julie could see he was well over six feet tall. "I'd like to take you to meet Mother now, if there are no more questions. Please don't let her frighten you."

Julie said, "But I do have another question."

Unbelievably there was a smile on his face as he led her out of the study. There was even a touch of warmth to those cold eyes. "Yes?" he prompted her.

"I was wondering whose portrait is hanging in the library," she said, returning his smile with one of her own.

But his smile quickly vanished. "That, Miss Jacobs," he said, "is my loving wife."

He walked briskly down the hall, leaving Julie no choice but to scurry after him.

CHAPTER FIVE

Julie's new employer rushed up a
beautiful spiral staircase with lightning
speed. But she caught up to him as he
paused to knock gently on one of the
second-floor doors. Then he opened the
door for them to enter.

Mrs. Bigelow's opulent suite was the
complete opposite of her son's monastic
study. Here everything was pink and
white, plump and swathed in silky material, including Mrs. Bigelow herself. She
lay on a pink divan propped up on several pillows, wearing a pale dressing
gown dripping with lace, her white hair
piled high on her head. Plump fingers
and arms sparkled with jewelry as did
her tiny pink ears.

"You must be Julie," she said, ignoring
her son, who stooped to kiss her cheek.
Her blue eyes gleamed with interest as
she held out both arms and pulled Julie

toward her. "Do sit down beside me, dear, and let's get acquainted. Brad, do stop fidgeting. Either sit down somewhere or be on your way. I must talk to this young lady." She cocked her head to one side. The blue eyes looking at Julie were suddenly a little bit surprised. "You know, I think she bears a striking resemblance to Amy."

"Amy?" asked Julie, but no one paid the slightest attention to her.

"Mother," Brad said warningly, "let's not talk about Amy."

"You know, Brad, Amy might very well still be here if you had a little of your late father's financial genius. She might not have disappeared if you'd have made a really big killing on the market. Girls like her want more than just a comfortable living."

"Now, Mother, haven't I always provided? Don't you have everything you want? Things are going very well for us. Everyone assures me that I'm managing the family estate as well as can be expected. I'm in the process of having two new office buildings constructed downtown, and I'm looking into the possibility

of a couple of shopping malls in the sub-
urbs. That's where I feel the new growth
is going to be. We're comfortable, Mother,
but I think the day of the big financial
coup is over."

Julie was amazed at the change in this
man called Brad. The self-assured voice
she'd encountered downstairs was now
pleading, and his demeanor reminded
her of a small boy seeking adult approval.

"Comfortable? As well as can be expected? Namby-pamby words. Your father knew how to do things in a big way.
Life was fun with him. You'll never be
half the man he was."

Julie tried to read Brad's eyes. For a
second she thought she saw pain in
them, but all they reflected now was a
cold, stony look.

"Mother, Miss Jacobs should not be
subjected to this family talk. I'll leave
you alone so you can explain her duties."

"Of course. You must get back to tele-
phoning those stodgy advisers of yours."

The plump, pretty face blew him a kiss
of dismissal, and he hurried away, again
reminding Julie of a small boy.

"Hard to believe a son of Chester Bige-

low could be so dull and unimaginative."
The old woman leaned toward Julie as if
sharing a confidence with a friend.
"Don't let his good looks take you in.
He's a cold, unfeeling fish."

Unsure how to react, Julie began to
giggle nervously.

After a moment, Mrs. Bigelow joined
in. "I think I'm going to like you, Julie
Jacobs," she said.

"And I'm going to like working for you.
I know I am," Julie replied sincerely.

The duties Mrs. Bigelow outlined to
Julie appeared light, nothing like the
way they had sounded when discussed by
her son. There should be plenty of time
to use that library, after all.

Several times Julie noticed Mrs. Bigelow's blue eyes studying her face quizzically. She wondered if that had anything
to do with the portrait in the library and
decided she'd ask as soon as there was a
break in the monologue. Julie never got
the chance, for they were interrupted by
a tap on the door.

The fat maid Julie had encountered in
the entrance hall stood in the doorway
holding a tiny white Pekingese with a
pink ribbon in his hair.

"Oh, Molly, bring the baby to Mama." Mrs. Bigelow held out her arms just as she had for Julie.

Then the dog was hugged and covered with kisses. He settled down on his mistress's lap, looking a little embarrassed.

"Show Miss Jacobs to her room, Molly, and help her unpack. I'll see you at dinner, Julie, at six o'clock sharp."

Julie followed Molly to the doorway, where she looked back at the two pink-and-white figures on the divan in the pink-and-white room. She hated to leave this haven of warmth and affection—the only place she'd felt welcome since arriving.

Then she remembered Brad Bigelow's words: "Don't let her frighten you." What could he possibly have meant?

CHAPTER SIX

Julie reached the dining room early, proud that she'd been able to follow Molly's directions without getting lost, for this house was larger and more complicated than anyplace she'd ever been. The long, gloomy halls she'd passed through had done little to alleviate the feelings of nervousness and depression that had overtaken her as she'd unpacked her belongings.

Surrounded by affluence, she longed for the comfort of her plain little room at home, the smell of her mother's freshly baked bread, and the sound of her father's whistling, none of which could ever be hers again.

The only other person present in the long white-and-gold dining room was Brad Bigelow, who wasted no time on greetings.

"Where is my mother?" he asked as soon as Julie walked through the gilded archway.

"Why, she told me she'd meet me here," Julie stammered. That was what she'd said, wasn't it?

"It's your job to escort my mother wherever she goes, including to dinner. I would think you'd realize that, Miss Jacobs. After all, you have been employed as her companion."

Julie looked into the glowering black eyes and swallowed. She could feel the heat rising in her face and knew she must be turning red. Before she could think of an appropriate reply, Mrs. Bigelow swept into the room in a lovely gold caftan that trailed across the plush carpet making a soft swishing sound. (Did she always match her surroundings? Julie wondered.)

"Stop bullying her, Brad. Julie is doing just what I told her to." Mrs. Bigelow linked arms with Julie, who could feel her nervousness melting away in the presence of this lady's warmth. "Now, where is Dan? That boy is never on time. Well, never mind. He'll be along. Why

don't you fix us a cocktail? I'm sure Julie
must be feeling a little anxious on her
first night here."

Julie gave her a grateful smile, but
said, "Nothing for me." Drinking was
something she'd had very little experience with. She certainly wasn't used to
having a cocktail before dinner every
day.

Mrs. Bigelow gave her a pat and
swished off toward Brad. Julie stood
awkwardly twisting the ribbon that
served as a belt on her homemade dotted
Swiss dress. Brad's eyes told her it was
inappropriate, and once more her self-
confidence was beginning to fade.

The sudden appearance of her red-
headed antagonist from that afternoon
added to her self-consciousness. Why
should the gatekeeper be entering the
Bigelow's private dining room?

"Well, if it isn't the princess, and
wearing a sweet sixteen dress, too.
Charming," he drawled.

Julie's embarrassment grew. She
wished she could disappear.

"Dan!" Mrs. Bigelow said. "At last
you're here. Let's be seated so the staff

can begin serving. They do so hate to be
off schedule." She seated herself at the
foot of the long table set with gold-
rimmed china.

"Miss Jacobs, this is my cousin, Daniel," Brad began formally, but Dan didn't
wait for him to finish.

"I've met the lady," he said, "and I
think I can guess why you chose this par-
ticular one, eh, Brad?"

Brad's dark eyes bored into Dan's, but
he said nothing as he seated himself at
the head of the table and rang for the
serving maid.

Julie's place was opposite Dan.
Throughout the meal, he needled her un-
mercifully and occasionally passed a
barb to his cousin. Brad remained detached and pompous except when ad-
dressing his mother, whom he treated
with great solicitude.

She, in turn, was a charming hostess,
chattering continuously about the soap
operas she evidently loved to watch and
about Pekos's (Julie surmised Pekos was
the Pekingese) escapades. She rejected
Brad's solicitude and jabbed at his pom-
posity. Julie was grateful for her pres-

ence and directed her own few comments in the woman's direction. Still, it was a relief when the meal ended.

During the next few days, Julie settled into the routine of the household and found her duties to be light indeed. She breakfasted with Mrs. Bigelow, then filled in the morning playing chess, doing needlework, or reading to her charge. The mornings passed pleasantly enough in this dear woman's company.

After lunch, however, Mrs. Bigelow settled down to rest and watch the afternoon soaps, leaving Julie to do pretty much as she pleased. A romp with Pekos, a walk on the grounds, and, of course, books from the library helped fill in the time until dinner.

Mealtimes were repeat performances of the first, the only variations being the new plots explored on the soaps and the new exploits of Pekos. Mrs. Bigelow's evenings were filled with more TV, Pekos, endless poring over fashion and movie magazines, and the continuous ordering of caftans, robes, and gowns.

Julie tried hard to be of service to the woman. But since her presence was frequently not required at all, she began to wonder why she had been hired. Obviously, this household could function just as well without her. She hated to admit it, but she was bored. Bored and homesick. What had started out as a great adventure was rapidly turning into a lonely humdrum existence.

Her first day off aroused mixed feelings in Julie. It would be good to leave the grounds, which she had explored until she knew every nook and cranny, but she would miss the companionship of her patient, limited as it sometimes was. At breakfast, there seemed an inordinate amount of interest in her plans for the day. Even Brad was less withdrawn and more human than usual.

"Do take a walk in Delaware Park," Mrs. Bigelow urged. "Down by the lake. It's so pretty there."

"Yes, you are looking a little pale, Miss Jacobs. It will do you good to get out," said the man who had warned her that he was not to be involved in making plans for her day off.

"The park is majestic enough to please even royalty like yourself," Dan added, but his smile took the sting out of his words.

"The park across the street it will be," Julie said gaily. "It appears unanimous, anyhow."

"I'll have Mrs. Fynn see that cook packs you a little lunch, dear," Mrs. Bigelow said.

Julie gave Mrs. Bigelow a grateful look before running back to her room to change from her skirt into slacks. Molly was straightening the room and wistfully remarked that it was a grand day for a walk in the park. Julie agreed as she quickly changed. Then she dashed down the stairs, taking a moment to pick up her lunch before she was off.

And it was a grand day. The sun was warm, the park green and lush, the time seemingly unlimited. The morning was spent exploring the park's historical museum, which had many rooms.

Julie ate her lunch on the back steps overlooking the lake, then set off on a narrow path running along the lake's edge. As she ducked overhanging branches and slid in the damp earth underfoot, she began thinking about the household she had left behind that morning. There were so many unanswered questions in her mind.

Why had Brad hired someone to look after his mother, when she needed so little care? And why had he hired someone who looked like his former wife? What had happened to that wife? Why had he warned her about sweet Mrs. Bigelow? Why did Dan Bigelow work as a gatekeeper at the mansion?

Julie was eager to find answers to these questions. The quest should relieve her boredom.

She had seen no one else on the path, but suddenly there was a sharp crack behind her, as if someone had stepped on a dry twig. Twisting her head to look back, she felt a sharp blow at the base of her skull. Whirling spirals of pain enveloped her, and the ground appeared to be rising toward her. She tasted mud in her mouth and felt cool water lapping at her feet. The roaring in her ears grew louder and louder, and then she felt and heard nothing.

CHAPTER SEVEN

Julie woke up in her own room with a throbbing head. Gingerly she raised it from the pillow and, when nothing worse happened, cautiously sat up on the edge of the bed. Slipping into her embroidered blue robe, which was lying conveniently across the foot of the bed, she stood up.

For a moment nausea overcame her, but then it began to subside. Walking across the thick carpet in her bare feet, she swung open her door, which was un-latched. A soft murmur of voices drew her attention to two figures bent toward each other in complete absorption.

Although the corridor was dim, there was no mistaking that shock of red hair or the gray-clad, mothball-scented woman—Dan and the housekeeper. What could they be discussing so se-cretly? Julie felt it had something to do with her, but then she told herself that was merely because they were near her room. She stepped into the hall, closing the door behind her. The faint click as the door latched made the two jump apart guiltily, or so it seemed to Julie.

Dan walked toward her in a perfectly normal manner, a wide grin of relief on his face. "Julie, how are you? I'm so glad you're awake, but shouldn't you be lying down? Let me help you back to bed. You know, you scared me to death. I've called Dr. Palmer. Come on now." He took her hand gently and led her back into her room. "When I found you, I thought you were dead."

"You found me?" Julie was confused. "What happened?"

Dan sat her on the edge of the bed and covered her with the hand-crocheted afghan she had brought from home. "The doctor should be here any minute. Please take it easy. Yes, I found you. I went over to the park to meet you, and it was lucky I did! I wasn't sure where you'd be, but I guessed the museum. I saw you on the steps, but before I could get to you, you started down the path. I followed, but you had a good head start. Then I thought I heard a thud up ahead. Only, I wasn't sure. A few minutes later I found you lying at the edge of the water."

"Why were you going to meet me? You don't even like me," Julie blurted out.

The look that passed across the freckled face was unclear. Then the face was pressed close to Julie's, and she realized she was being soundly kissed. Her emotional feelings were mixed with physical pain, for the base of her skull, where his hands were entwined in her hair, was very tender, and he was making the throbbing much worse.

It was with embarrassed relief that Julie heard the bedroom door open. Dan tried to turn casually, but Julie noticed he was flushed and nervous as the two of them faced the three people staring at them.

Brad Bigelow was tight-lipped, with both anger and hurt in his eyes.

I suppose he can't believe a cousin of his would stoop to consort with the help, Julie thought.

Mrs. Fynn appeared frightened. It was the third person, however (Julie guessed he must be Dr. Palmer), who displayed the most emotion. Julie watched his jaw drop and saw moisture glisten on his upper lip as his face grew pale.

The mild blue eyes behind round glasses showed disbelief. "I—I didn't know..." he faltered as he swayed a little in the doorway.

"Dr. Palmer, this is your patient, Julie Jacobs. She's Mother's new companion." Brad was as formal as ever, seeming not to notice Dr. Palmer's state or Julie and Dan's embarrassment.

Brad's words seemed to steady the doctor, who took the black bag Mrs. Fynn handed him from the hall. He slowly walked toward Julie.

Meanwhile, Brad ushered Dan and Mrs. Fynn outside, saying, "We'll wait in the hall, Doctor, as we're anxious to have you check Miss Jacobs's condition."

Julie was left alone with the odd little man. She tried to remember what Mrs. Bigelow had told her about him. He seemed too mild and unassuming for a multimillionaire. Mrs. Bigelow had mentioned that he was a very wealthy widower with a beautiful daughter and, as

Julie gazed at this short, balding man whose trembling hands were working the short zipper on his medical bag, she decided the daughter must surely have taken after her mother.

Dr. Palmer looked into her eyes with an ophthalmoscope, and Julie knew he was checking for signs of increased intracranial pressure. He also checked her grip, her reflexes, and her ability to answer simple questions. He had her stand by the side of the bed, heels and toes together and eyes closed, to see if she could maintain her balance. Pulse and blood pressure were also checked.

As he put away his equipment, he said, "You were lucky, Miss Jacobs. I believe that branch did nothing more serious than give you a mild concussion. Some pain tablets and rest should have you feeling fine in no time."

"What do you mean, branch? I was hit with a branch?"

"Why, yes. Dan told me on the phone that a low, heavy branch had gotten caught back in a tree and your passing somehow dislodged it. It must have sprung forward and struck you at the base of the skull, knocking you down."

So that explained it. But how could a big branch get pulled and trapped backward? Probably someone had pushed it there to clear the overgrown path. The footsteps she'd heard must have been Dan's. The snap, the sound of the branch as it popped out of its place of entrapment. Julie felt relieved as she took two headache tablets. It was a silly freak accident, nothing more. She thanked the doctor, told him good-bye, and was preparing to sleep when the door flew open and two familiar pink-and-white creatures swept in.

Pekos reached Julie first with a little leap. His wet kisses told her he was glad she was okay. Mrs. Bigelow was right behind him. She sat on the edge of the bed enveloping Julie in her plump arms.

"My poor baby," she sighed. "How could that Brad let this happen to you? I knew I should have gone with you."

Julie tried to imagine Mrs. Bigelow hiking through the brush in one of her glamorous outfits. "But, Mrs. Bigelow, Brad had nothing to do with it. It was my day off and a silly accident happened.

Don't blame Brad and don't blame yourself."

"Of course, of course," Mrs. Bigelow
agreed, but then looked like a naughty
child about to spill a family secret. "But
why do you think Brad hired you?" she
asked impishly. "Why did he ask for a
photograph?" The blue eyes probed
Julie's.

"I'm—I'm not sure. I did wonder about
the photo, but I think he hired me because I was the most qualified. At least I
hope so," she finished lamely.

"Don't believe it," Mrs. Bigelow said.
"He had over one hundred applicants, all
with photos, and he chose the one that
looked like Amy."

"Who is Amy?" asked Julie, repeating
a question that hadn't been answered before.

"Amy, my dear, was Brad's wife. One
day they quarreled and she disappeared
and hasn't been seen or heard from since.
Do you wonder that I worry about you?"

Julie leaned back against the pillow
and closed her eyes, letting Mrs. Bigelow
babble on. Brad had nothing to do with
her accident. It was odd that he had

hired a look-alike for a companion to his
mother, but that was all it was—odd.
Still, she would have liked to know more
about his motives. Sometimes he did
scare her.

Mrs. Bigelow seemed to have read
Julie's thoughts. "Oh, now I've frightened you. Of course, Brad wasn't involved. I shouldn't have said anything
with you all bumped and bruised like
this. Now don't you worry about a thing
and don't pay any attention to an old
woman's ramblings. I've asked Dr.
Palmer to stay right here until I'm sure
you're okay again. I'm not going to let
anything happen to you, no siree."

And after a few more hugs and kisses
from both Mrs. Bigelow and Pekos, Julie
was left alone.

The pain pills were making her
groggy. She wanted to sit up and think
about what Mrs. Bigelow had said, but it
was too much of an effort. At one point as
she was fighting sleep, she thought she
saw Brad's piercing eyes glaring at her.
She made an effort to speak, but the eyes
disappeared and she fell into a heavy,
troubled slumber.

CHAPTER EIGHT

Next morning when Julie awakened, she touched the back of her head gingerly. It was still tender, but the intense aching was gone. Her mouth was dry and foul-tasting, and her eyes were crusted with what her mother always called "sleepy dirt." Both conditions were remedied by her usual morning ablutions.

As Julie donned a simple green sundress and white sandals, she recalled someone talking to her several times throughout the night, pushing at her eyelids and hurting her arm. It must have been Dr. Palmer, she decided, checking her pupils and blood pressure. Her memories were all mixed up, containing bizarre dreams, pain, Dan's kiss, Brad's eyes, Mrs. Bigelow's insinuations, and the interruptions during the night.

Julie was trying to sort it all out when there was a knock at the door.

Molly looked surprised to see Julie up
and about. "I was just going to ask if you
wanted a breakfast tray, miss, but you
don't look like you'll be a-needin' one.
How are you feeling?"

"Pretty good, Molly. The head's a bit
cloudy but much better."

"You best be careful, miss. We don't
want anything happenin' to this pretty
lady."

The faint emphasis on "this" made
Julie ask, "Molly, did you know Mrs.
Brad Bigelow?"

"Yes, ma'am. I did. If you don't mind
my sayin' so, you resemble her extraordi-
nary. In the kitchen everyone is marvel-
in' that we should have two ladies as
alike as peas in a pod here at the mansion, one right after the other. But where
you're always sweet and sunny, the
young missus was—well, sorta sad and
discontented like."

"Where did she go, Molly? What do
you think happened to her?"

Julie knew she had asked one question
too many when Molly stiffened.

"You best be asking that of someone
else, miss. After all, I'm only the maid."

With that she flounced down the hall.

Standing alone in the room after the rebuff, Julie felt ashamed. Unused to servants, she must have crossed the line from appropriate to inappropriate behavior. Would she ever learn? Slowly she went to see to Mrs. Bigelow.

When she turned into Mrs. Bigelow's suite, she noticed Dan with Mrs. Fynn again, so preoccupied in conversation that neither one noticed her.

A few minutes later when Julie and Mrs. Bigelow left the room, there was no one in sight. Her curiosity was aroused, but she had learned from her experience with Molly, so she said nothing to the white-haired woman who was chatting a mile a minute at her side.

The breakfast gathering was larger than Julie had anticipated. Because it seemed that Dr. Palmer was now a house guest. He seemed over his shock of yesterday (Bet he thought I was Amy Bigelow, Julie thought), and greeted her cordially, inquiring in a medical manner about her injury.

Mrs. Bigelow kept asking him if he was sure Julie was all right, while patting Julie's hand protectively. He assured her that she was. Brad remained the cool host. He asked the right questions politely enough, but in a distant, uninterested manner. He looked disapprovingly at Dan's usual late entry but changed completely when a gorgeous blonde entered a few minutes later.

"Sophie, how delightful you look," he said with a smile. "This is Dr. Palmer's daughter, Sophie," he said to Julie.

Sophie did look delightful. She had on a honey-colored linen dress that Julie, with knowledge gained from looking at Mrs. Bigelow's endless magazines, guessed came from a Paris designer. It just matched her long honey-colored hair, which sported a pair of sunglasses on its elegant, sleek top.

"Thanks, Brad," Sophie said carelessly to the man Julie was amazed to see holding her chair for her. No such courtesy had ever been extended to Julie.

The conversation was dominated by Sophie, who seemed not to notice that the males were hanging on her every word. For that matter, Mrs. Bigelow gave every indication of being fascinated by the beauty in their midst as well. Only Julie was bored and left out.

Suddenly, as if reading her mind, Dan turned to Julie and gave her a broad wink, while his fingers squeezed hers under the fancy tablecloth. And she felt better for his efforts.

"Brad, why don't you show Sophie the back garden? It's so pretty now that you've finally gotten a gardener to spruce it up. And a stroll is a perfect aid to digestion," Mrs. Bigelow said, pushing back her chair and rising to leave the room. She called back to Julie, "Find a good book and Pekos and meet me on the front porch. I'd like to make sure that you're getting fresh air and rest at the same time."

Julie had to smile. This patient of hers gave her no chance to protest. She just disappeared quickly, a practice Julie had watched her use successfully before, when she wanted to maneuver the household members to get her own way. Brad, especially, was often duped by this practice, but he never seemed to realize it. Julie, on the other hand, was very much aware of what was going on. But

since she was not averse to Mrs. Bigelow's present plans, she turned toward
the door.

"I'll come with you," Dan said immediately.

But before he could, Mrs. Fynn appeared in the doorway. "May I speak to
you a moment?" she asked in her no-
nonsense voice.

Dan looked at Julie and shrugged,
then nodded to Mrs. Fynn. As the two
walked away, Mrs. Fynn turned in
Julie's direction, giving her a smug, tri-
umphant look.

Surprised, Julie stood still a moment.
"What's this all about?" she murmured.
"What's going on between Dan and Mrs.
Fynn?"

"Why, didn't you know? She's his
mother."

Julie whirled around, and there sat
Dr. Palmer, all but hidden in a corner,
smiling at her.

"She's his mother," he repeated.

CHAPTER NINE

The next few weeks flew by in a happy haze for Julie. There could be no mistaking Dan's obvious infatuation with her, and Julie's romantic nature enjoyed his attentions immensely. It wasn't that she was in love with him. There hadn't been time for that. But after their contentious beginnings, it was nice to be singled out as the recipient of his friendly gestures.

His mischievous teasing made her laugh and reduced her boredom. She had learned a lot about this stocky, muscular fellow with the shock of red hair in the short time since they had called a truce. His flashy exterior hid a sweetness and consideration that reminded her of Jim. But Dan's flair for the dramatic was his alone. He flopped on the couch rather than sitting, swung on a door rather than merely opening it, and collapsed on

49

the ground rather than lying down. He could easily be aroused to anger, flying off the handle over insignificant matters, and was apt to slam doors, kick inanimate objects, or hit something when mad. He was bold and brash and somehow lovable.

Julie tried to dismiss the one remaining cloud over their friendship, namely Dan's neat sidestepping of any questions regarding his relationship with the housekeeper. His natural exuberance would be suppressed following any such question, and when Dan felt bad, it removed a bit of brightness from the lives of all those who came in contact with him.

For this reason, Julie found herself not mentioning what she'd learned from Dr. Palmer. Still, the attachment slowly flourished, with the members of the household reacting in a variety of ways.

Mrs. Bigelow appeared pleased and constantly gave Julie light duties and extra free time. Whether this was to aid the romance, or because she was so wrapped up in Sophie and the planning of activities for Sophie and Brad, Julie was uncertain.

Brad, on the other hand, was unmistakingly against the match, no matter how tenuous it might be. Whenever he saw them together, he glowered.

He invented new duties for Julie. "Take Pekos downtown and get him groomed," he ordered. "Catalogue the books in the library." When all else failed, he said, "Doesn't Mother need you for something?"

Julie always hurried off obediently to do his bidding, but secretly she was delighted she was bothering him. After all, she was only doing what he had told her she must: finding her own source of entertainment during her free time.

Mrs. Fynn also disapproved, but her disapproval took the form of silent watching, pursed lips, and withering looks. Sometimes the discovery of her silent form, exuding that mothball scent, watching the two of them together would send goose bumps up Julie's arms.

Dr. Palmer remained indifferent. So did Sophie, for the most part, although occasionally a look of amused disdain flitted across her beautiful face. Dan's personality seemed to draw females to him, and at mealtimes Sophie was often

more interested in his humor and conversation than in Brad's more serious
words. Thus, Julie decided, the disdain
must be for her.

The one person wholeheartedly enjoying the romance was Molly.

"It's just like in the movies, Miss
Julie," she remarked one day, delivering
a bouquet of wildflowers Dan had given
her for Julie's room. "You've found yourself a good man."

"He's just a friend," Julie replied as
she put the flowers in a little white vase,
thinking how like Dan they were, carefree and unregimented, bursting with
life and color. "Don't be getting ideas,
Molly."

Molly gave her a broad wink before
going out the door.

Julie changed into a pair of green
shorts and a white shirt with a frog
print. Next she brushed her hair, and
then, on impulse, pinned some of the
wildflowers among the waves. As she
looked at her reflection in the mirror, she
saw that her eyes were sparkling and
her cheeks glowing at the prospect of
meeting Dan in the park. She applied

some lip gloss and grabbed a tote bag packed with a book, a softball, and some munchies. She was hurrying toward the door when the intercom buzzed imperiously.

Oh, no, she thought, but she answered, "Yes?"

"Miss Jacobs, I know Mother dismissed you for the day, but I want you to take Pekos for a walk. He really hasn't been getting enough exercise lately." Brad's voice crackled over the wire with just a hint of accusation in it. "And, of course, you're to be back for dinner at the usual time."

"Of course, sir. I'll be glad to," Julie answered obediently.

She smiled to herself. She liked the little dog's company, and since she was going to the park anyhow, walking him would entail no change in her plans. She thought of Brad, picturing the dark, brooding look in his eyes. He remained an enigma to her, but his discomfiture regarding herself and Dan reduced him to a more human level.

With Pekos on his leash, Julie hurried to Delaware Park, this time going nowhere near the lake, but instead making the long trek to a concession stand, the agreed-upon meeting place. Before she reached it, however, Dan came bounding up to her, cradling a football in his large, freckled hands.

"Hiya, doll," he said, then gave her a kiss that missed her lips and landed near her chin. "We're playing a little touch football." And he jogged back to a group of boys ranging in age from about eleven to twenty.

Julie was amused. Dan enjoyed sports and the company of other young men interested in sports. He was majoring in physical education at Baker College and wanted to be a football coach when he graduated next year. They never went to the park that he wasn't surrounded by a scraggly bunch with whom he patiently worked.

That was why Julie had gotten into the habit of bringing a book. This time she didn't read it, for the group was soon breaking up with Dan, flopping on the grass beside her.

His eyes told her he admired how she looked in her shorts, but his lips said,

"Where'd you get that crazy frog shirt?"

"My mom made it for me," Julie said.

Pictures of her pretty mom, who was always doing something for one daughter or the other, filled her mind. She saw her hunched over the yards and yards of material that eventually became Doreen's wedding gown, icing the girls' yearly birthday cakes, sitting patiently and proudly at all the school events the two of them participated in, and then waving happily from the car window as she and Dad left on their first vacation in ages.

To Julie's embarrassment, tears began rolling down her cheeks. She was crying, something she hadn't done in months. Why now? Why in front of Dan?

Dan was embarrassed, too. He hugged her uncertainly and tried to distract her the way one does a small child. "Look at Pekos. He's chasing a butterfly."

Julie looked, but she only sobbed harder.

"C'mon now. People are looking at me like I'm beating you," Dan said softly. "Look, would it help if you talked about your mother, Julie?"

Julie could tell he really didn't want to listen to that.

"No," she said, and then, to her own amazement, added, "It would help to talk about yours."

Dan pulled away from her as if stung, picked up the tote bag and Pekos's leash, and started across the park. "Let's go," he said brusquely. "It's almost time for dinner."

Julie knew that it wasn't, but she stumbled along behind him, feeling ashamed that she'd touched his vulnerable spot just because she'd felt so vulnerable herself. She wiped her face with the back of her hand. Something fell to the ground. Looking back, she saw the little clump of wildflowers, no longer bright and cheery but wilted and crumpled.

The sun still shone. The park was still lush and green. But the afternoon's bright promise was gone.

CHAPTER TEN

"Mrs. Bigelow, is Mrs. Fynn really Dan's mother?" Julie asked one morning, trying to sound casual.

Mrs. Bigelow didn't appear surprised by the question. "Why, yes, dear. She was married to a distant cousin of my late husband's, but he died when Dan was ten. From what I understand, money was always a problem, but she managed to raise him alone in Albany through high school. After that she desperately wanted to send him to Baker College, but she couldn't find work. She remembered her husband's rich cousin and came here to see if we could help her find a job and a place to live near the school."

"But why is her name Fynn and Dan's Bigelow? Did she marry again?"

"Oh, no. When she came here, she was using the name Bigelow. But there were

already two Mrs. Bigelows in residence
at the time, myself and Amy, so she took
her maiden name, Fynn. Of course, when
Brad found out she was a relative, he
didn't want her to work as housekeeper.
He offered to let her stay on as a guest
and promised to help with Dan's education, but she flatly refused. And rightly
so, I might add. Penniless distant rela-
tives have a habit of turning up at one's
doorstep and can be quite a nuisance.
She has worked out well enough as
housekeeper, but I'm sure Brad pays her
an exorbitant wage for her special brand
of slinky service."

The sting was taken out of these last
words by the now-familiar giggle. Julie
suspected that much of what was said
was simply for effect, but the word picture so aptly described Mrs. Fynn that
she had to join in the merriment. The
light interlude was short-lived, however,
for Julie's memories of those shadowy
hallway meetings between Dan and the
housekeeper halted her laughter and
prompted her to ask, "But why does Dan
hide their relationship?"

Mrs. Bigelow shrugged, her interest

waning. "Pride, I guess. I don't know. He is a proud lad in some ways, but not too proud to take the money Brad gives him every week, though he puts in little enough time as gatekeeper."

Julie recalled her first meeting with Dan, the gatekeeper, and had to smile again. Like Pekos and the pampered fat feline from next door, they had hissed and growled at each other, showing their dislike in the very arch of the back and the tilt of the head. Also, like Pekos and Kitty, after they had gotten used to each other, they had become pals, playfully teasing each other, exchanging an occasional snap or swat, but usually content to sit side by side in the sun.

Now she had ruined all that. Was it because of pride? Had she injured Dan's pride by questioning him about his background? Or had it been the way she had asked him? He had been trying to help her and she'd turned on him. She didn't know why he'd been so upset. But she did know she wanted Dan back to his former happy-go-lucky self.

"What were you thinking about?" Mrs. Bigelow was peering at Julie curiously, for she had become so lost in her thoughts that the embroidery she'd been doing was about to tumble to the floor.

"Pride. I was thinking about pride."

"Oh," Mrs. Bigelow said, "like pride goeth before a fall?" Then her dimples popped into view as she giggled again at her own joke.

The two were in Mrs. B.'s sitting room, their embroidery floss scattered over the settee, the remainder of their midmorning tea on a cart in front of the nearby white fireplace. Julie looked at her patient swathed in a pale-blue dressing gown, hair piled on top of her head, ropes of pearls draped around her plump neck, and smiled warmly. She realized how fond she was of this puckish little lady, and how much she had missed their pleasant mornings together, which had been greatly curtailed since Dr. Palmer and Sophie had been persuaded to spend part of their vacation at the mansion (a recent development).

"Hand me last night's *News,* dear," Mrs. B. said as she put aside the linen napkin she'd been working on. "I think I saw an item about a promising young artist showing at the Albright-Knox Art

Gallery beginning today. I want to clip
the article out, as I'm sure Brad will
want to take Sophie. Maybe you'd like to
go sometime, too," she added as an after-
thought.

Apparently she found what she
wanted in the paper, for she began busily
snipping with her embroidery scissors.

"I don't know much about art." Julie
smiled as she tried to picture Dan in an
art gallery. It would be rather like the
proverbial bull in a china shop, she decided. Unbidden, a mental image of Brad
with the glamorous Sophie on his arm,
standing before a painting, flashed
through Julie's mind and her smile vanished.

"Good morning, ladies."

Julie flushed deeply, for the face she'd
been picturing was now smiling at her.
"G-good morning," she stammered.

"Hello, dear." Mrs. Bigelow was smiling at Brad with none of the rancor
usually reserved for him. In fact, Julie
noted, since Sophie's arrival, Brad was
seldom attacked by his mother's acerbic
tongue. "Would you like a cup of tea? I'll
ring for a fresh pot."

"No thanks, Mother. Just thought I'd

drop by to see how you're doing. And as I don't see much of Miss Jacobs anymore, I thought this would be a good opportunity to see how she's doing, also."

"Where's Sophie?" The older woman's voice was a trifle sharp as she watched her son moving embroidery floss in an effort to find a place to sit on the settee.

He shrugged indifferently as he lowered his large frame onto the dainty couch. "Miss Jacobs, have you completely recovered from your unfortunate incident?" He turned his attention to the still embarrassed Julie.

Mutely she nodded.

Now Mrs. Bigelow's voice was sharp as she interjected, "Brad, you've just got to take Sophie to the Albright-Knox to see the new exhibit there." She waved the clipping in his direction. "You two have so much in common," she added in a more normal tone.

"Maybe Julie would like to see it, too."

Julie was as surprised by his use of her first name as by his words and warm smile.

"Oh, Dan can take her anytime, but Sophie's time is limited. Besides, Julie knows nothing about art. Do you, dear?"

"No—" Julie began.

"No time like the present to learn then, is there?" Brad said, gazing warmly into her eyes.

Julie was staring back transfixed when Sophie swept into the room.

Although casually dressed in white slacks and a pale-blue silk blouse, Sophie looked as lovely as ever. Her sleek blond hair was in a pageboy without a single unruly strand breaking the perfection of its smoothness. Her nails were rounded at the ends and glowed with a pale polish. Her creamy complexion looked so natural that it didn't seem possible she could be wearing makeup, but Julie had seen the many bottles and jars on her dressing table.

Sophie glided over to Brad with cool assurance and, standing between him and Julie, said, "So this is where you've gotten to, darling. I've been looking for you. Father tells me there's an exhibit at the gallery that we should see." Putting her arm through his possessively (for he had risen on her entrance), she ignored Julie, but turned to Mrs. Bigelow brightly. "You'll let me steal your son for a little while, won't you?"

"I've just been suggesting the very same thing," Mrs. Bigelow replied, beaming at the couple. "How wonderful that you happened by."

Brad seemed about to protest, then allowed himself to be propelled to the door. "You sure you don't want to join us, Miss Jacobs?" he asked as Sophie was pulling him out of sight.

"No, that's all right. Have a good time." Julie felt silly talking to the empty doorway.

"Don't they make the handsomest couple?" Mrs. B. was beaming again.

"Yes, they do," Julie agreed, feeling a sharp stab of disappointment at missing an exhibit she'd never heard of before this morning. Resolutely she picked up her embroidery. "Yes, they do," she repeated.

CHAPTER ELEVEN

The day had dragged for Julie. Brad and Sophie must have lunched somewhere near the gallery. Dan was working at the gatehouse. Mrs. Bigelow took a tray in her room.

That left Julie and Dr. Palmer in the dining room, and Julie found the mild-mannered man almost impossible to communicate with. He didn't actually ignore her. In fact, she could feel him staring at her when she was preoccupied with her salad. But whenever she looked at him, he quickly averted his glance, a strange, sad look on his face. She felt sorry for him without knowing why.

Then she inwardly laughed at herself. Imagine a poor country girl feeling sorry for a millionaire.

When the meal finally ended, Dr. Palmer disappeared into the recesses of the large house after a few meaningless pleasantries.

Julie had spent the afternoon in the library cataloguing some of the books as Brad had once suggested. She enjoyed running her hands over the fine old bindings of the classics and guessing at the stories contained within some of the newer volumes. When she tired of these occupations, she curled up in a chair with an old Agatha Christie. The mystery, which she'd read before, failed to hold her interest, but she plodded on. Later, though, as she prepared for dinner, it was with a certain amount of anticipation. At least she would be with people.

Julie thought of Dan and wondered if he was still annoyed or hurt because of her prying. She hadn't meant to upset him. Her thoughts drifted to Brad and his new, friendlier attitude. What had caused such a change? Unbidden, a picture of Sophie, her hand on Brad's arm, her lovely face smiling up into his as they set off for the gallery, filled Julie's mind. Of course, that was it. Brad was in love, and love was beginning to mellow him.

She slipped a navy sailor dress over her head and was tying the bow at the collar when there was a hesitant knock on the door. Julie opened it.

"Mrs. Bigelow is wantin' you to stop by for her on your way to dinner." Molly stood there uncertainly. It was unusual for her to bring such a message since Mrs. B. was in the habit of using the intercom.

"Yes, Molly. Is there anything else?"

The maid hesitated, flushed, then blurted out, "I know it's not you, but Mr. Brad I should be talkin' to. But if she finds out, she'll be makin' my life miserable."

"Who, Molly? If who finds out?"

"Why, Mrs. Fynn, ma'am."

"Mrs. Fynn? What's happened involving Mrs. Fynn?"

"Well, I'm hatin' to say this, miss, but I happened to see her in Mr. Brad's office this afternoon, and it was most peculiar. She was just goin' through his desk like a house afire. When she saw me lookin', she pretended she was straightenin' things. But she was snoopin'. I know she was, and I know I should tell Mr. Brad. But she can be a mean one, that Mrs.

Fynn. Oh, yeah. She can be a real mean one." The plump, honest face wore a worried look.

What in the world could Mrs. Fynn be looking for in Brad's desk? Julie wondered. "I'll take care of it. Don't worry," she said to Molly, though she had no idea how she would carry out this promise. The look of relief on Molly's face convinced her she'd made the right decision. "Just leave it to me," she added more firmly as she slipped into white sandals and followed Molly out the door.

Mrs. Bigelow was waiting in a flowing blue-and-gold gown. She embraced Julie, then linked arms with her and started for the dining room. Julie was tempted to tell her about Mrs. Fynn, but as much as she loved this dear little lady, she felt her too frivolous for a confidante.

Mrs. B., on the other hand, appeared to want to confide in Julie. Slowing their pace in the darkening hall, and lowering her voice, she said, "I'm so pleased that Brad is taking an interest in Sophie at last. I've always hoped it would work out between those two."

Julie nodded unenthusiastically. The

round face that peered up at her in the hall's gloom was suddenly unfamiliar, the shadows changing its contours.

"I do hope nothing comes up about Amy's strange disappearance. The police can be so bothersome. Brad was lucky he was able to get the investigation stopped, but—"

"Investigation? Police?" Julie stopped completely. A tightening of her chest muscles was making it hard to breathe.

Mrs. Bigelow pulled her forward. "Oh, yes. They were quite sure Brad had murdered her, but no body was ever found. That Amy always was uncooperative," she added with a giggle, a giggle that hung oppressively in the air as they entered the dining room.

Murder! Julie thought. What kind of a place was this? What had she gotten herself into when she answered that offbeat ad? She tried to force herself to breathe more normally.

The faces looking at her as she made her way silently to the table all seemed different tonight. Mild Dr. Palmer looked sly; cool Sophie looked knowing; Dan, who had not been the same since she'd asked about his mother, looked secretive; Brad, hard and mean. Only Mrs. Bigelow, now that she was again in the light, looked the same. Like a robin, Julie thought, watching Mrs. B. bobbing up and down as she twittered to each one in turn.

Watching her, a giggle began to form in Julie's throat, a hysterical giggle that she was able to suppress, but which was followed immediately by a familiar dull thud over her right eye, the first signal of a migraine

Oh, no, she thought as she sipped some water. It had been months since she'd had one, but she knew that without rest and quiet, it would progress in intensity until it was unbearable and she was reduced to a sick, wretched mass.

Dr. Palmer's clinical eye must have noted something, for she heard him say, "Are you all right, Miss Jacobs?"

"I—I have to lie down. I have a migraine," Julie murmured.

The twittering robin turned into a mother hen. "My poor dear. What a shame. Let me take you to my room. It's closer."

Julie would have smiled at the sudden reversal of the nurse-patient roles if her head hadn't been throbbing so.

"I'll send up some Midrin. I have some in my bag." Dr. Palmer was standing up. "You're not allergic to anything, are you?"

Julie replied negatively and assured him that Midrin was what she usually took.

Despite the constant clucking and twittering, Julie was grateful to Mrs. Bigelow for getting her out of the dining room and back to her suite in a matter of minutes. A faint smell of mothballs permeated her consciousness and made her nauseated.

She lay down on the divan and Mrs. B. placed a cold washcloth over her eyes, just as her mother had always done. Julie squeezed her hand in thanks.

There were footsteps, voices whispering, and more footsteps, which only made the pain more severe. Please go away, Julie thought. Go eat your dinner before it gets cold. Go discuss the day's happenings or your problems or whatever, but please go.

"I'll send Molly to stay with her." That was Brad.

Then Sophie said, "Is that really necessary? She only has a headache."

Had they all followed her? Yes, they must have, for now Dan's voice was saying, "It's not just a headache. It's a migraine, which is quite a different thing. Oh, here's Molly now."

Julie could imagine the disdainful look Dan probably gave Sophie.

Mrs. Fynn was there, too, saying, "I left her medication from the doctor in the cup on the table."

There was more murmuring and rustling, but at last they were leaving.

Blessed silence reigned, broken only by Molly's soft voice. "I'll just be gettin' you a drink of water to take your medicine, miss." Then, "Here you go."

Julie reached out her hand and lifted her head, washcloth still in place. Her head felt as if it were in a vise, as though the scalp were too small for its contents.

Molly placed three small pills in Julie's hand, which she transferred to her mouth, then reached out again for water. With the glass halfway to her lips, she sensed something was wrong and spit out the pills, ripping the washcloth from her eyes.

"Molly, these can't be my pills," she said. "Midrin are capsules." Then she began to vomit.

CHAPTER TWELVE

"I'm sorry. That line is still busy. Would you care to try a little later?"

The cool impersonal voice annoyed Julie, but she managed to answer politely. "Thank you, operator. I will." Maybe she should forget the call, she thought. Things did look different today.

After she'd stopped vomiting last night, Molly had given her the Midrin, which she'd found in an identical plastic medicine cup on the same table where she'd picked up those three blood-pressure pills of Mrs. B.'s.

"Land's sake, Miss Julie, I can't figure out how this got pushed under the edge of that stack of movie magazines. Lucky you knew the difference."

At the time Julie had just swallowed the capsules gratefully and lain back with her cool cloth, while Molly sat be-

74

side her in the dark (light always made her headache worse), massaging her forehead.

She'd finally dozed for a half hour and, as so often happened if she could get to sleep during an attack, awoke pain free. Knowing that the family would soon be leaving the dining room, if they hadn't already, she hurried to her own room. She had given Molly instructions to say that she was fine, that she was going to sleep and would not like to be disturbed.

But she had not slept. Mrs. B.'s words about Amy, "They were quite sure Brad had murdered her," reverberated inside her head until she feared they'd bring on another attack. In an effort to block them out, Julie concentrated on the medication mix-up. Why had three blood-pressure pills been left on the stand? Julie herself doled out Mrs. Bigelow's medication, and her dosage was one tablet daily at eight A.M. Who would have taken out three tablets?

Julie toyed with the idea that maybe the mix-up had been deliberate, rejected it, then returned to think about it some more. Dr. Palmer had taken her blood pressure after her concussion, so he knew it ran low. He would also know that three of Mrs. B.'s strong pills would surely make her sick to her stomach if nothing more.

That's foolish, she told herself. Three tablets of that dosage all at once would be enough to make most anyone sick. And certainly with all the people milling around in that small room, anyone could have found the opportunity to make the switch.

Once on this tack, she tried to remember who was there, but that was no help since everyone, except Molly and Dr. Palmer, had wandered in. And Dr. Palmer had sent the medication and Molly had given it, so even they couldn't be eliminated entirely. Of course, cook and Sarah, the quiet little serving maid, had remained below (at least Julie had no evidence that they hadn't). But other than that, it could have been anybody. Who would want to harm her and why?

These questions were unanswerable, but they made Julie think of Mrs. Fynn, who clearly didn't like her. And that made her think of the mothball smell that had made her nauseated when she entered Mrs. B.'s quarters. Mrs. Fynn must have been in the room earlier. Why? Julie could only guess at her reasons, and that made her wonder about Mrs. Fynn snooping around Brad's office, and that got her thinking about Brad, which inevitably got her thinking about his wife and those awful words Mrs. B. had mentioned so lightly—words like murder, police, and investigation.

So there she was, back at square one. And that was how it went all night. Finally she had worked herself into such a state of fright that she'd checked the lock on the door three times and promised herself she was calling Jim early in the morning.

When the first rays of the morning sun crossed Julie's windowsill, she was sitting by the window in a white wicker rocker feeling a little silly. Just as the dark shadows of her room were being chased by the spiky fingers of light, so were her suspicions of sinister plots beginning to vanish with the dawning of the new day.

She had been a nurse long enough to know the realities of medication errors among professionals—where elaborate safety precautions were observed. Nosiness was nothing new, either. She thought of the two spinster sisters who had lived next door to the Jacobs family for years. Dad had joked about the two so lacking in excitement in their own drab lives that they'd resorted to peering through the slats of their venetian blinds at any signs of activity next door.

Dad had joked, but he had also invited them to numerous barbecues, birthday celebrations, and get-togethers, showing his usual understanding and compassion for others. Perhaps she should show a little of the same understanding to Mrs. Fynn.

Julie had dressed quickly, putting some cover-up makeup over the dark circles under her eyes, and taken a tray with Mrs. B. in her room. She didn't feel like facing the whole group as yet.

When she gave her patient her blood-pressure pill, she had asked as casually as she could, "Do you know who could have left three of your pills in a cup on your stand? I, uh, noticed them last night."

"Why, I did, dear. On your day off I never let Molly give me my pills. I take them myself, but with my arthritis, I sometimes have trouble and pour too many. You mentioned that one should never put medication back into the bottle, so I just save them till your next day off, although I do usually put them in my drawer." She paused for a moment. "Now don't you dare scold me, you nurse-person, you."

Julie looked at the pouty mouth and burst out laughing. She should have known.

Now as she waited to place her call to Jim again, she realized that someone could have deliberately switched the cups, pushing hers under the magazines, but it seemed pretty farfetched. Still, it would be nice to have someone familiar and solid from home around, someone she understood and trusted completely. She was going to ask Jim to drive up and that was that. Resolutely she picked up the phone, and this time she got through.

The sound of Jim's voice sent waves of

homesickness through Julie. The trembling of her hands and of her own voice made her realize how much she had suppressed her feelings for her roots. Jim was delighted to hear from her since he'd sent her several letters and she'd only managed one.

Of course he could drive up; in fact, he could leave within the hour and would be there by late afternoon. Of course, he would give her love to Doreen and Mark and, of course, he missed her, too.

It was only after she'd hung up that Julie realized she'd forgotten to ask permission for this visit. As if on cue, Brad Bigelow walked into the library. Julie sprang away from the phone guiltily, for she hadn't asked to use it. What was wrong with her today? She was usually so conscientious, had even instructed her family never to call unless it was an emergency. Well, this was an emergency, she told herself.

Brad interrupted her thoughts by saying formally, "I hope your headache is gone, Miss Jacobs." Then he seemed to notice those not-very-well-covered circles under her eyes, for he walked over to her and gently touched them, making her face tingle.

He murmured, "Poor little girl." Before she knew what was happening, he tilted her face up and tenderly kissed each eye. Then he stood there looking down at her.

Julie could hold the guilt no longer. No matter that what her employer had just done was not exactly good manners either. She didn't think of that. She was too concerned with clearing her own conscience.

"I'm sorry I used the phone without permission," she blurted out, "but I did reverse the charges." He looked at her curiously. She hurried on, "And is it okay if a friend visits me for the weekend?"

He looked surprised but managed a calm, "I think that might be a good idea. Would you like to have her share your room or should I have Mrs. Fynn prepare another?"

"It's not a she. I mean, he's not a she. She's a he—I mean, it's a man." Julie was embarrassed.

Brad was silent for a moment. "Make the arrangements with Mrs. Fynn," he said finally. "I can't be bothered with all this." He turned on his heel and left.

All alone, Julie touched her cheeks, her eyes. Had he really touched her? Had he actually kissed her? She felt euphoric until a wave of depression hit her. Had she really acted like such a fool?

CHAPTER THIRTEEN

"Princess, there's some guy at the gate here who says he's your boyfriend. Since that's a title I've been sorta trying for, I thought I'd check with you. Says his name is Jim." Dan's voice over the intercom made Julie smile.

"For a guy in contention for a title, you sure haven't been around much lately. Better give someone else a go at it. Let him in," she said lightly.

There was a long pause. Then, "Okay, princess. Guess you know what you're doing."

A few minutes later, Julie was hugging and kissing Jim at the front door. As she stood back and looked at him, the frightening suspicions of last night seemed very foolish indeed.

"Let me show you to your room," she said, "since it's almost time for dinner,

83

and Brad—I mean Mr. Bigelow—hates unpunctuality."

Jim raised an eyebrow at the use of her employer's first name, but made no other reference to it. Instead he said, "Quite a place you're working in, honey. Don't think I can afford anything like this after we're married." He pulled her tightly to him and kissed her again. "Will it matter?"

Julie was annoyed. He'd been here less than five minutes and already she felt stifled by his possessiveness. "Aren't you taking me a little for granted, Mr. Wick?" she managed to ask mildly as she disentangled herself from his embrace.

The hurt-puppy look as he said, "Sorry, hon," immediately made her contrite. Taking his hand, she smiled and led him to his room: a warm and inviting place due to the efforts of Mrs. Fynn, who was checking the bathroom linens as they entered.

For the first time since knowing her, the housekeeper spoke to Julie with something less than malice in her voice.

"I think you'll find everything in order, Miss Jacobs," she said, the corners of her mouth bending up ever so slightly.

Julie said, "Why, thank you, Mrs. Fynn. It looks lovely."

The uptilt of the woman's lips increased, very much resembling a smile before she withdrew from the room.

What brought that on? Julie wondered. She dismissed Mrs. Fynn from her thoughts and turned to Jim. "Now tell me about everything back home."

She heard all about Mark and Doreen's new puppy with the crooked nose and the floppy ears, all the town gossip that Jim could remember, all about the Shaber sisters, who had lived next door to Mom and Dad and were now making constant excuses to visit Doreen, much to Mark's chagrin, and all about Jim's job.

All the time they were talking, Julie was thinking of the years she'd shared with this young man, the years of their high-school days. He was smart in school, and so was she. That may have been what had attracted them to each other in the first place, but it grew to be much more than that. He was reliable, serious, and popular, president of their class in the senior year and also good in some of the sports.

He wanted to be a lawyer one day and,

with his thick glasses, he did look the part. He was working in a law office at present, while continuing his studies, and his earnest attitude would surely lead him to his goal. His devotion to Julie had never wavered since the time he had taken the school bus with her, always carrying her books. Yet their romance had never sparked somehow. Could things like that change? There was still no spark now.

"Why don't you freshen up?" she asked Jim after glancing at her watch. "I'll come back in a half hour and take you down to dinner where you can meet everyone."

Dinner did not go as Julie had hoped. She had worn a favorite pink-and-white-checked skirt with a puffed-sleeve blouse. But she wished she'd chosen differently when Sophie made her entrance. The willowy blonde wore a white silk creation that dipped to a vee both in front and back, revealing some lovely, well-tanned skin and drawing a certain amount of attention.

Jim seemed mesmerized by the blond beauty, and Dan, who had previously seemed indifferent to her charms, could not show her enough attention. Sophie, for her part, flirted outrageously with both of them, while Julie felt like a true country bumpkin.

That appeared to upset Mrs. Bigelow, who kept expounding on Julie's virtues. Julie appreciated her well-intentioned concern, but wished she'd just remain silent. Dr. Palmer watched his daughter affectionately, but said little, though he occasionally stole sidelong looks at Julie, a habit that rattled her.

Brad, reserved as usual, directed a few polite remarks to both Sophie and Julie, but for the most part remained detached. Watching his handsome, aloof profile, Julie couldn't believe he'd ever looked at her tenderly and called her a "poor little girl." Had that actually happened this morning?

"We really should leave on Monday," Dr. Palmer was telling Mrs. Bigelow. "I can't be dragging this vacation out too long."

That's the day after tomorrow, Julie thought, the same day Jim leaves. She found herself not unhappy at the thought, but whether that was due to the impending departure of Jim or of Sophie, she didn't try to analyze.

"You must see the Albright-Knox," Sophie said to Jim over dessert. "Brad and I found it delightful, and there was the nicest little cafe where we had lunch. Great paintings, great lunch, and great company, right, Brad?" Her artfully made-up eyes were leveled at Brad, who merely nodded agreeably.

"Don't know much about art," Jim said, shoveling in huge bites of the apple cobbler cook had prepared that morning.

"There's no time like the present to learn then, is there?" Sophie asked, giving Jim the full eye treatment.

Taking advantage of the Jim-Sophie conversation on art that ensued, Dan leaned toward Julie and whispered almost inaudibly, "Do you really think he'll fit into palace life, princess?"

CHAPTER FOURTEEN

Sunday was rainy and gloomy. After lunch Mrs. Bigelow settled down to watch a movie matinee on TV, so Julie took Jim exploring through the house, beginning with the basement. After descending a center stairway, they took a right turn that led them into a cool area under the kitchen.

Here there was a fruit cellar. And next to it was a partitioned-off space that had been turned into a cooler. Nearby was the door leading to the subbasement wine cellar. But Julie did not show Jim the wine cellar, for she was reasonably certain the door was locked.

Instead she took him to the photographer's darkroom that looked as though no one had used it in years, and an exercise room filled with stationary bicycles, a rowing machine, barbells, a punching bag, and other equipment. A duffle bag that Julie recognized as belonging to Dan had been carelessly thrown in one corner, its contents spilling out on the floor.

Pekos, who was touring with them, found this room to his liking and tore around at great speed, only to stop, reverse his direction, and proceed in the same manner the opposite way, all the time yapping as if to say, "Look at me."

Julie and Jim enjoyed his antics until, eventually, tired of his game, he picked up a golf ball from Dan's bag and carried it with him as they continued on to the game room. This was a room Julie had occasionally frequented with Mrs. Bigelow. It was the one place in the house where Mrs. Bigelow definitely didn't blend in with her surroundings. The oversized leather furniture was far too masculine for her flowing robes, ribbons, and jewelry. Julie and her patient had played chess here and worked some jigsaw puzzles, but Mrs. B., perhaps realizing that she was out of her element, preferred the upstairs rooms for most of their diversions. Jim, however, liked the game room immensely and spent a lot of time poking through the shelves, which were bending under the weight of every kind of game imaginable.

Next they peeked into the laundry area, a vast section used mainly by the staff, which also contained the furnace room.

Across from the exercise and game rooms was a bar area, complete with poker and pool tables, which hadn't seen action for a long time.

This had been Chester's hangout, Mrs. Bigelow had told Julie with pride. "He and his cronies would be down here till all hours, but Brad's stodgy friends don't know how to enjoy themselves."

Julie tried to imagine Brad in these surroundings as Jim dropped a ball into a side pocket and Pekos dropped the golf ball on her toe. But Jim seemed to fit no better here than Mrs. B. did in the game room. Off the bar was a bathroom, more utilitarian than glamorous, but immaculately kept under the supervision of Mrs. Fynn.

"That concludes the downstairs tour," Julie said as she put Pekos's golf ball

back in the exercise room. She and Jim
had fallen into an easy, friendly relationship after their rather inauspicious beginning the previous evening. They had
spent the morning chatting about old
times and also trying to sort out their
feelings. Julie still felt there was no
spark between them, but there was a
genuine friendship, an understanding.
That conclusion left her relieved but sad,
and she wondered how Jim felt.

"Gee, Julie, I can't believe people
really live this way. I mean, think of the
upkeep alone on this place." Jim's major
emotion at the moment seemed to be one
of awe—awe at the power of money.

"And you ain't seen nothing yet," she
told him lightly. "Follow me."

Julie led him up the stairs to the main
floor. The tour here went rather more
quickly, for Jim had already seen some of
the rooms on this floor. He expressed a
desire to see the portrait in the library,
which Julie had told him about in her
one and only letter.

"It's uncanny," he said. "The resemblance between her and you is fantastic."
He stood in front of the picture for a long

time, running his fingers through his short sandy hair. "Well, so that's the former mistress or whatever of Bigelow Manor. She's a dead ringer for you, Julie."

She could tell that Jim's lawyer-like cogs were turning, that he was wondering, as she had, why Brad would hire someone who looked like his wife to work at the mansion.

Finally he said, "Wasn't there something you wanted to tell me? Something that was bothering you? I thought that's why you asked me here, and I keep expecting you to bring it up, but you never do."

Julie led him up the stairs and past the second-story sleeping quarters. "I was just homesick, I think," she said slowly.

All the fears she'd entertained so seriously just a couple of days previously no longer seemed valid. Even Mrs. B.'s dramatic announcement about Amy Bigelow's mysterious disappearance had lost most of its impact.

"Life is so different here, so erratic and full of emotional upheavals that I guess I needed to see someone solid and steady from home," Julie went on. "Now that you've come, I'm beginning to understand that I've been caught up in a new lifestyle here and maybe having a little trouble adjusting. You've changed my perspective," she added as they continued up to the third floor where the rooms were smaller. "Servants' quarters," she told him, "maids, cook, gardener, and Mrs. Fynn."

She remembered the curtain moving at a third-story window on the day of her arrival. Must have been Mrs. Fynn, she thought. Wonder why it bothered me after all those years next door to the peeping Shaber sisters?

They didn't look at any rooms on the third floor but headed up the stairs for the top story where they were met by some closed double doors.

"Now for the grand finale," Julie said, and she flung the doors open.

"Holy cow," was all Jim managed to say.

But there was no disguising his look of pure astonishment as the two of them gazed at the large fourth-floor ballroom, a ballroom with a polished parquet floor and three huge crystal chandeliers.

Impulsively Julie put her arms around Jim's neck, and the two of them whirled up and down the length of the gorgeous room, Pekos yapping at their heels.

"Just like high school," Julie said as they leaned against the wall in exhaustion.

That set them off laughing until their sides ached. For their shabby school gym had been nothing like this magnificent room.

"Seriously, though," Julie said, "doesn't this ballroom make you wonder about its past? Bet there were a few shindigs held here in Chester's day."

They linked arms and, to Julie at least, there came visions of former inhabitants of Bigelow Manor decked out in their finery, bowing, chatting, and waltzing across the parquet floor. Why, she could even picture a giant punch bowl at one end of the room. Here Chester held court, surrounded by a wild crew of cronies, telling a few indiscreet stories out of the hearing of the ladies, throwing back his head and laughing uproariously.

"Julie." Jim wasn't involved with her

fantasies. He was gazing worriedly at his watch. "Honey, weren't we supposed to meet the others at four P.M.? It's twenty to right now."

Julie jumped back to reality. "Oh, dear, and I have to shower and change out of these grubby clothes. There was more dust in parts of the basement than I realized. Let's hurry."

They did hurry. A short time later, a refreshed Julie, feeling self-confident in a pink linen sheath, linked arms again with Jim before entering the downstairs game room. Mrs. Bigelow had insisted that, since all the guests were leaving Monday morning, they must do something "fun" this afternoon.

Julie and Jim found Mrs. Bigelow in charge of the proceedings, with everyone scurrying to and fro procuring the ingredients necessary for her "fun."

"That's right, Brad," Mrs. B. was saying. "Get the glasses from the bar and set them on the coffee table. Sophie, tell Mrs. Fynn to send Molly down with the hors d'oeuvres."

Sophie saluted sharply in a svelte sailor playsuit, and Julie knew she'd chosen her outfit incorrectly again.

"Doctor, set up that card table. You help him, Dan, and get out the cards. Where's the champagne?" She spotted Julie and Jim. "Hi, you two," she called out gaily. "Could one of you find somebody to get a bottle of champagne?"

"I'll do better than that. I'll get it myself," Julie said merrily, caught up in the excitement.

She knew how Mrs. Bigelow missed the freewheeling days she'd enjoyed with Chester. It was good to see her enthused and involved in something other than the soaps and Pekos. Humming a little tune, Julie ran up the stairs and asked Mrs. Fynn for the wine-cellar key.

"It's unlocked," Mrs. Fynn said sourly. She obviously didn't share in the general high spirits.

Julie bounced back down the stairs, listening to the hubbub from the game room on her left. She opened the door leading to the subbasement wine cellar. Then she stood at the head of the stairs trying to remember where the light switch was. All at once there was a sharp thump in the middle of her back, the bang of the door slamming, and then she was falling down the stairs.

CHAPTER FIFTEEN

Hurtling down in the darkness, Julie
reached out blindly and caught at a railing which stopped her plunge, but not
before she'd torn her dress and skinned
both knees. She sat down on a step to
assess the damage and pull herself together. She could feel the blood oozing
through torn stockings, and her right
elbow, which had scraped along the wall,
stung. She was about to try standing up
when the door opened and a light flicked
on.

"What happened?" Brad was looking
down at her.

"Someone pushed me." Julie began to
shake.

Brad ran down the steps and carefully
helped her to her feet. "Thank heavens
you didn't fall all the way," he said fer-
vently. "That would have been deadly."

Julie looked at her blood-stained linen dress. "I should have worn a playsuit," she said irrelevantly and began to cry.

Brad took her firmly by the shoulders. "Tell me exactly what happened," he said sternly.

Julie told him everything.

He looked relieved. "A draft must have blown the door shut. I think that's what struck you. There are strange currents in this basement. I should know. I played here often enough as a child."

"Why do these things keep happening to me? Am I becoming accident-prone?" Julie sounded almost hysterical.

"Two little accidents don't make you accident-prone, Miss Jacobs. As a nurse, you should know that. Just be thankful, as I am, that nothing more serious has happened."

Easy for you to say, Julie thought, but remained silent.

He patted her absently, noticed the blood, and gently wiped most of it away with his handkerchief. His thoughts seemed elsewhere as he helped her to the top of the stairs.

"Wait right here," he said, "and hang

on to that door. I'll get the champagne."

As she waited, Julie accidentally pulled the door toward herself. The knob struck exactly where there was a very tender spot in her back. So he was right, as usual, she thought. The door had hit her. She spent the remainder of her waiting time trying to picture Brad Bigelow as a child but found the task impossible. One thing she was sure of, however. He would have been a very handsome child indeed.

Back with a bottle of champagne, Brad helped a very stiff Julie into the game room. They could hear the revelry before they arrived. Rock music was blaring, mingled with much laughter, so much that no one noticed them standing in the doorway for several moments. Sophie was dancing, not a hair out of place, with a willing but uncoordinated Jim for a partner. Dan and Molly stood by the card table clapping in time to the music and laughing. In one corner Mrs. B. and Dr. Palmer were jitterbugging.

Brad took one look and gasped, "Mother!"

The action stopped as all eyes turned

toward the doorway taking in Julie's be-
draggled appearance. So much for tonight's entrance, Julie thought ruefully.
Jim crossed to her immediately and took
her in his arms, where she promptly
burst into tears again. Dan turned down
the radio, and everyone demanded to
know what had happened.

Brad explained quickly, then asked,
"What were you thinking of, Mother? A
woman of your age and condition dancing like that." He turned to Dr. Palmer,
who reddened and held up his hands as if
to ward off an attack. "And you should
certainly know better!"

"She hasn't harmed herself, Brad. We
just started dancing a couple of minutes
ago. Besides, exercise is good for the
heart. I wouldn't do anything to hurt
Daisy. You know that, Brad."

Brad didn't appear to be convinced.
Julie had the feeling he didn't really like
Palmer though he was always polite to
him.

"Julie, dear, why not get changed and
let Dr. Palmer look at your wounds?"
Mrs. Bigelow said, her blue eyes full of
worry. "Brad, stop fussing at me and let's

take care of this poor child. Young man, take her right to her room."

Dan started forward, but Julie wiped her eyes and waved him back. "I don't need the doctor," she said. "These are only scratches. Jim will help me take care of them. Start your card game and we'll be right down."

Back in her pretty room, Julie burst into tears once again. "There, there," Jim said, peering at her earnestly through his glasses. "It will be all right."

"Oh, Jim," she sobbed after she'd taken off her torn stockings in the bathroom, "I keep having these accidents and I get so frightened. I'm so glad you're here. I don't want you to go. Do you think you could stay another week or two?"

"Tell me about the accidents," he said calmly as he went to work washing her cuts.

Listening to herself, Julie had to admit it didn't sound like very much when it was all spelled out. The cathar-sis of the telling was more helpful than anything else. She left out one thing—the accusations against Brad—and for the life of her, she didn't know why.

"Am I getting paranoid?" she asked Jim when she had finished.

"Of course not," he said slowly. "You've been through a lot lately, under a lot of strain. A new job, first time away from home, entirely different way of life, and then these incidents. They all do have logical explanations, though. I really do think they're accidents, hon. But if it'll make you feel better, I'll call the office first thing in the morning and see if they can do without a very junior staff member for a week or two. After all, I do have some vacation time coming up."

"Thank you, Jim. It really would mean a lot to me." Julie hugged him again, looked sorrowfully at her dress, and grabbed a pair of pedal pushers and blouse from a hanger, then ran into the bathroom to change.

Downstairs, Brad, Sophie, Dr. Palmer, and Mrs. B. were finishing a canasta game while Dan strummed on a guitar. Julie and Jim sipped on some champagne (after what it cost her, she felt she deserved a little of it), then joined the group in a long game of Monopoly. Brad was the big winner almost from the start.

Before they knew it, it was time for their late dinner.

As they picked up the play money and the little houses and hotels, Mrs. Bigelow said, "Oh, Julie, while you were upstairs, I finally persuaded the Palmers to stay a little longer. That means more fun times in the future."

"Good," Julie replied, smiling, and realized she meant it. It pleased her to see Mrs. B. enjoying herself so much. "That will give us a chance to take revenge on your son, the wicked owner of Park Place."

Brad actually flashed her a smile, a smile that lit up his whole face. He was still wearing the remnants of it when a flustered Molly appeared at the door.

"Mr. Brad, there's someone here to see you."

"A visitor? I'm not expecting anyone. Who is it?" Brad looked puzzled.

Molly hesitated, not meeting his eyes.

"Who is it, Molly?"

"It's—it's Miss Amy."

CHAPTER SIXTEEN

After Molly made the startling announcement that Amy had come to the house to see Brad, Mrs. Bigelow was the first one to recover her composure.

"Run along, Brad," she said. "The rest of us'll go on up to dinner." Her calmness was surprising considering her great hopes for a Sophie-Brad romance.

A red-faced, tight-lipped Brad hurried out of the game room, while Dr. Palmer suddenly became rather pale and agitated.

Dan appeared amused for some reason. Or so Julie thought.

As for herself, she felt a great sense of happiness. Now at least she knew for sure that Brad Bigelow hadn't murdered his wife. The living proof was right here in this house.

However, as the group went upstairs

and walked toward the dining room, Julie's spirits sagged a bit, for Brad could be heard shouting in his study.

"Blast it, Amy! I won't have this! Get out of here. Get out, right now!"

No more could be heard once Julie was inside the dining room, but Brad's tone of voice had been truly frightening.

The only one, seemingly, with an appetite was Jim. Totally bewildered by what was happening, he attacked the food on his plate with his usual enthusiasm, now and then smiling reassuringly at Julie or peeking surreptitiously at Sophie. The glamorous blonde seemed to hold the same fascination for Jim that some exotic creature from the zoo might have held. That was the way Julie saw it.

Or was it possible that he had a genuine personal interest in the wealthy doctor's daughter?

Sophie, for her part, paid no attention to Jim tonight. Gone was her earlier flirtatious manner. Instead, she was very sulky, eating little and looking frequently toward the door, as if to will Brad back into their midst. It was the first time Julie had seen Sophie without her air of cool indifference, and it made her rather vulnerable and human.

Dan always enjoyed the theatrical. He tapped his fingers impatiently beside his plate, an expectant look upon his face, as if he couldn't wait for the next act of tonight's drama to begin.

Dr. Frank Palmer, meanwhile, had become a man to be pitied. Ashen and shaky, he nervously pushed his mashed potatoes around his plate with his fork. "Perhaps we shouldn't stay after all," he said, looking pleadingly at Mrs. Bigelow.

"Nonsense," she answered. "It's all been settled, and I'm not going to let Amy ruin my plans. It's time this place was filled with people and good times again. Why, tonight was the most fun around here in ages."

No one said anything for a long while, and the silence stretched uncomfortably.

To break the tension, Julie finally spoke up. "Jim and I went to the fourth floor today. There must have been some grand parties in this house at one time."

"Indeed, there were," Mrs. Bigelow said merrily and was off again remin-

iscing about the many splendid parties
and dances that had been held at the
mansion when she was younger.

Even Sophie showed some interest.
"Were there fabulous gowns?" she in-
quired.

"Oh, my dear, yes." Mrs. B. began de-
scribing the fantastic creations adorned
with seed pearls, lace, beads, and even
feathers. "Of course, Chester always saw
to it that I had the most gorgeous dress
of all," she added proudly. "In fact, most
of my old gowns are stored under the
eaves in the turret at the far end of the
ballroom. I'll have to show them to you
girls." Excitement was making her
cheeks pinker by the moment.

"I know what I'm going to do," she
said. "I'm going to give a ball, a little
ball for just us and Brad's associates.
We'll have an orchestra and—yes, we'll
have a ball next Saturday."

"But that's not enough time!" Even
Dan, who was never practical, could see
the difficulties in this venture. "There
would be so many preparations to make."

"Pooh," said Mrs. B. "You've never
seen me in action, and I have Julie to

help me. It's not as though we have a lot
of invitations to get out. We'll just telephone Brad's friends."

"That doesn't give them much time to
arrange their schedules. They may have
made other plans." Sophie also was un-
convinced of the practicality of the plan.

"They're simply not that type of people. Can you imagine Homer Shaw having to check his social calendar before
making a commitment?" Mrs. B. raised
an eyebrow in a comical manner.

Apparently those acquainted with
Homer agreed. Even Frank Palmer managed a slight chuckle, though he still
looked like a sick old man.

"I'll get an orchestra and arrange for a
catering service to handle the food, since
our staff is now so small," Mrs. B. continued. Julie wondered if this, too, was a
reflection on Brad and his handling of
the household as compared to the invin-
cible Chester. "We won't serve dinner,
just lots and lots of refreshments."

Mrs. B. made plans happily right
through dessert.

With the meal finally over, the group
filed out into an empty hall, where there

was no longer any shouting to be heard. They went into the seldom-used formal living room with its Oriental carpets and its fragile French provincial furnishings. The powder-blue walls, combined with the dampness creeping into the house from the continuous drizzle outside, cast a pall over the group, including Mrs. B.

Dan, as out of place in this dainty room as the proverbial bull in a china shop, tried to take over the duties of host in Brad's absence. He poured and passed out some after-dinner drinks in tiny stemmed glasses. Then he settled himself rather uncomfortably on a fragile antique chair, raised his glass, and smilingly said, "Here's to Mrs. B.'s ball. May it be fit for a queen."

They all raised their glasses obediently, but they soon began drifting off, and Julie was sure they were all wondering, as she was, what was happening in that study down the hall.

CHAPTER SEVENTEEN

That night Julie had a strange dream. She was skipping down a pathway strewn with flower petals in a beautiful garden. The sun was shining, birds were singing, and she was filled with happiness. Eventually she noticed a closed door in a tall wall that seemed to surround the garden. Feeling like Alice in Wonderland, she slowly pulled the door toward her and peeped through, yet she could see nothing but blackness.

She stepped closer to the doorway, hoping to catch a glimpse of something. Then bang! She felt a thump in her back, heard the slam of a door, and felt herself falling down, down, down.

As she fell, she heard the door reopen, and through it came hands—big hands holding tiny stemware, little hands, ugly hands, hairy hands—and all the fingers

111

were reaching out for her. Julie wanted to scream, but she was afraid that would help the hands to find her.

A soft voice began to murmur over and over, "Poor little girl, poor little girl." Then the murmur turned into an angry shout: "Get out. Get out, right now!"

That was when Julie awoke, sweating profusely. She tried to close her eyes again, but she couldn't fall asleep. Then she tried to read and found she couldn't concentrate.

Sighing deeply, she put on her robe and decided to fix herself some warm milk in the kitchen. Maybe that would help calm her down. The downstairs night-lights were so dim, it was positively spooky.

As Julie passed the library, she heard two voices. One of them belonged to Dr. Palmer—and the other one was totally unfamiliar, so it had to be Amy's. Julie didn't want to eavesdrop, but she was only human.

"You know I never felt right about any of it," Frank Palmer was saying.

The brittle feminine voice replied coldly, "Come now, I certainly didn't have to twist your arm. You were more than willing for me to leave Brad. You were downright eager to talk about my divorcing him and marrying you."

"Whatever I was then, it's over. I won't be part of it any longer. I've always suspected the truth. You never cared for me. It was the money you wanted. That was all. I realized fast enough that we could never have any kind of relationship or marriage. And I don't understand why you've come back. I gave you enough money to live more than comfortably, the only stipulation being that you stay away. At least from me."

Julie was stunned, but a lot of loose pieces began falling into place. Amy must have run off with Dr. Palmer, planning to divorce Brad and marry him. That was the solution to the mystery of her disappearance. It also accounted for Frank Palmer's excessive shock at the sight of Julie and at the reappearance of Amy. Did Brad suspect? Perhaps that was why he acted peculiarly to Frank Palmer.

Amy's voice rose. "If I'm not going to share in the Palmer millions, I'm sure as heck not going to lose out on the Bigelow money, even though it's not as much as I thought when I married it."

"You're a fool. Brad will never take you back."

"He's angry right now, but he'll forgive me. You see, he adored me."

I shouldn't be hearing this. I don't want to hear any more of it, Julie finally thought, and she scurried up the stairs again, forgetting about the warm milk. Before she could turn down the guest wing, however, a dark shadow loomed up before her, giving her an instant of fright.

"What is going on here, Miss Jacobs?" It was Brad.

"I—I had a nightmare and couldn't sleep. Thought I'd get some warm milk."

"Where is it? Did you drink it downstairs?"

"N-no. It was so dark and spooky, I got frightened and came back without it."

He smiled.

He thinks I'm a silly, frightened child, she told herself.

"I can't seem to sleep tonight either," Brad said, tucking her arm in his, "so I'll scare away the spooks, if you'll make two cups of that milk."

Now Julie faced a dilemma. "It probably doesn't work," she said. "I've never tried warm milk, only read about it." Please, dear heaven, don't let him go down there and find those two together, she prayed silently.

"Then it's time we checked it out," Brad said softly, pulling her toward the stairway.

Julie tried to make as much noise as she could, but it was difficult in her soft slippers. Finally she faked a stumble, skidded down two steps, and thudded against the railing. It didn't make much noise, but Julie prayed it would alert the two in the library below.

"Shhh," Brad said, taking her hand. "You don't want to wake everyone up. You'll be heating milk all night."

They started down the hall. "Hey, what's that light in the library over there?"

"I don't see a light," Julie said.

"Well, I do." Brad pulled her toward the library door.

Julie hung back, but as the door

swung slowly open, she breathed a sigh of relief. The room was empty. She was grateful for Brad's sake and also for Dr. Palmer's. She felt the poor little man had suffered enough for whatever part he'd played in the unpleasant business. Her heart went out to the lonely widower who had become the victim, no matter how willingly, of the scheming woman she had heard tonight.

"That's odd," Brad said, switching off the lamp. "I was the last one to go upstairs tonight, and I know all the lights were off." He shrugged. "Maybe there are other insomniacs on the loose tonight, Miss Jacobs."

"Maybe there are," Julie agreed. "We better get our milk before it's all gone."

The two hurried along to the huge kitchen where Julie quickly warmed some milk in a small pan. Soon she and Brad were sipping the milk from two mugs as they sat in rockers in front of the fireplace.

"There's something I've been putting off telling you, but I mustn't put it off any longer," Julie said. "Molly is worried because she caught Mrs. Fynn looking through your desk." She hesitated, not knowing how to continue.

To her amazement, Brad merely smiled. "Don't worry about that. I know all about it."

The employer-employee gulf that usually separated them was nonexistent as they sat sipping and rocking in this pleasant, unpretentious room.

"What was it like living here as a child?" she suddenly asked.

"Lonely," Brad said. "This was my favorite room."

"The kitchen?"

"It was the one spot in this whole place where a little boy was assured of goodies, warmth, and—and love."

His mother must have rocked him here, too, Julie thought. "Was this your parents' favorite room also?"

"They never set foot in it unless it was to give an order." He looked so vulnerable sitting there in his maroon robe that Julie was sorry she'd questioned him. "Mother was all wrapped up in her social life, her gowns and her jewels, her trips abroad, and Father—well, Father was all wrapped up in Mother."

Julie could picture the lonely little boy creeping into the coziness of the kitchen to find the nurturing he needed from one of the servants.

"Father was really something, though. The only word I can think of to describe him is swashbuckling. I wanted to grow up to be just like him." Lights began dancing in Brad's dark eyes, lights that died just as quickly as they had come. "I failed, though," he said. "I'm nothing like him and never will be. Dan, odd as it may sound, is more like my Dad than he is like his own. That's why everyone is drawn to him." He gave Julie a sidelong glance, then a rather embarrassed yawn. "I think you better add warm milk to your list of remedies, Nurse Jacobs. I'm so tired I can hardly keep my eyes open."

Julie jumped up, suddenly realizing it was nearly four A.M. She had been so engrossed in the adventure, she'd somehow forgotten the purpose of the mission.

CHAPTER EIGHTEEN

Julie awoke tired and sore. She had much to think about, foremost being the relationship between Frank Palmer and Amy. The memory of her middle-of-the-night chat with Brad was one that she wanted to tuck away and bring out only when she was alone with nothing else to do, so that she could enjoy the rare moment of shared intimacy to its fullest.

She retrieved Pekos from the kitchen garden where he was sent after breakfast each morning, and she made her way to Mrs. Bigelow's suite.

When Julie arrived, the sitting room was empty, but there were voices coming from the bedroom. Julie recognized the brittle voice at once as the one she had heard in the library. But it was the agitation in Mrs. Bigelow's that concerned her.

"You should never have come back—never! You cause nothing but trouble for me and for everyone. What could you possibly want now?" The old woman's voice cracked and shook.

Dropping Pekos, Julie hurried to her patient fearing the consequences of this emotional outburst. She was followed by a silent dog.

The dark-haired young woman, perched on the edge of the bed, continued without noticing Julie at first. "Why, I want to be with my husband, dear Mother-in-law."

"I'll have to ask you to leave for a few moments, while I care for my patient," Julie told Amy, using her most professional tone.

"And just who do you..." The words came to a stop as the two young women faced each other.

Julie had the advantage, since she was prepared for a look-alike. Nevertheless, she was unnerved to see her own face looking at her in disbelief. Amy's hair had some reddish highlights and was twirled into a French twist. And her mouth was larger, more generous than

Julie's. But the overall resemblance was astonishing, despite Amy's sour look (something Julie hoped she didn't have).

Amy whirled back toward Mrs. Bigelow. "Who is this?" she demanded, standing up.

"My nurse companion, Julie Jacobs. Julie, meet Amy Bigelow." Mrs. Bigelow had regained her composure and seemed to be enjoying Amy's present discomfiture.

"How do you do." Julie smiled politely, but added firmly, "I really must take care of my patient now. You'll have to continue your visit a little later."

Amy's dark eyes appraised her, then ignored her. "Who hired her?"

"Brad." Mrs. Bigelow's blue eyes danced as she watched Amy for any reaction.

"Brad?" Amy was puzzled. Then she smiled. "He must have really missed me to find a substitute, but he'll learn that this gal isn't easily replaced." She pointed a coral-tipped finger at Julie. "Especially by this little mouse." Amy twitched her hips in her tight slit skirt and made her exit.

Pekos scampered after her, stopping at the door to let out a soft little growl. Then he turned to face them, looking for approval.

"Our sentiments exactly," Mrs. Bigelow said, giggling like a little girl. "Thank you, Pekos, and thank you, Julie. I was surprised at your ability to stand up to that—that..."

"That person," Julie finished for her. "Think nothing of it. We nurses are tough. We take special courses in how to deal with surprise visits from daughters-in-law."

"I don't know how that—that person ever talked Brad into letting her stay here. At least she's not in the master bedroom," the old woman added quickly, as if she feared Julie might be wondering. "It's not her he wants, though."

She's thinking about Sophie, Julie surmised.

"Let's forget about her," Mrs. B. said brightly. "We have work to do if we're going to have a ball."

Julie spent the remainder of the morning making lists. No sooner did she complete one list than Mrs. Bigelow started her on another.

When she wasn't making lists, she was looking up phone numbers. She was grateful she didn't have to worry about Jim, who was being given his first lesson in art by the lovely Sophie, an invitation issued hard on the heels of a rejection she got from Brad for a morning of tennis.

"I'm a little tied up this morning," a preoccupied Brad had said, not meeting Sophie's eyes.

Immediately Sophie had turned those sultry eyes on Jim. "Then why don't we take in the art gallery?" she asked. "I assume Julie has to work."

Jim had looked at Julie before committing himself. She had nodded and it had all worked out for the best.

"Let's have lunch up here today," Mrs. Bigelow suddenly suggested.

Julie called Sarah on the intercom, and soon the two women were munching egg-salad sandwiches and sipping tea. Pekos danced around on his hind legs entertaining them. He went through his entire repertoire of tricks: shaking hands, "speaking," rolling over, playing dead, and begging. He got so much egg salad for his efforts that his little sides were bulging. Eventually he curled up and slept soundly at Mrs. B.'s side.

"You know, dear, I think I'd like you to read to me for a while, and then I'd like to nap like Pekos." The usually perky Mrs. B. was drooping.

"That's a good idea," Julie said, "and I know just the book, a Rex Stout. I'll run and get it from my bedside stand." As soon as she got up to leave, Pekos was yapping at her heels, his nap forgotten.

"Okay, okay," she said. "I'll take you down to the garden first and pick up the book on my way back."

With Pekos right behind her, Julie ran down the stairs.

Dan was standing at the bottom. "I'll put him out," he said. "I've been wanting to talk to you, but you're always surrounded by your entourage. This time you're not going to escape. I demand an audience. Wait right here."

Julie was sitting on the bottom step when Dan returned.

"Some throne," he chuckled. "Listen, princess, I like you. Things were going great for us. Then I kinda blew it in the park. About my mother..." He hesitated.

"I know about your mother," Julie said gently. "Did you really think that would matter to me, Dan?"

"Princesses very seldom end up with us commoners, especially with all the competition around here lately. They usually end up with the prince."

"Haven't seen many princes around here lately." Julie tried to keep her tone light. "Unless they're all masquerading as frogs."

"You may just find one at the ball," Dan said. "Anyhow, I sorta wanted you to grant me a royal pardon or something for—well, you know." He shrugged. "Well, I gotta hop off. 'Bye." And he hopped away, making a croaking noise.

Julie laughed. She realized what an effort this conversation must have cost Dan, and she was grateful they could once again assume their easy manner with one another. "'Bye," she said. "I do believe there may be a prince in disguise around here."

She ran up to her room, the image of Dan's impish face still with her. She bounced over to the stand, grabbed the mystery, and started toward the door.

A folded piece of paper fell from the book in her hands. Julie retrieved it and, without thinking, unfolded it as she hurried into the hall. She stopped, her face growing white, for printed in bold letters on that little piece of paper was an unpleasant message: GO HOME. YOU ARE NOT WANTED HERE.

CHAPTER NINETEEN

The mansion was in a state of frenzy all week. Preparations for the ball were in full swing, and the unfamiliar faces of the newly hired were in evidence everywhere. Julie felt more like a secretary than a nurse as she bustled around trying to check items off those lists she'd made.

Musicians were traipsing up and down the stairs, since Mrs. B. insisted on rehearsals in the ballroom. They looked fresh and happy as they carried their instruments up, but were complaining about fourth-floor ballrooms with what breath they could still muster on the trip back down.

By Friday the flowers began to arrive, and the catering people were constantly in and out of the kitchen, much to the dismay of a usually unruffled cook.

Ordinarily Julie would have been beside herself at the prospect of going to a real live ball, her first ever. Instead, she was feeling forlorn. After receiving the ugly note, which she believed might have come from Amy, she had been wondering what to do.

Now she had made her decision. As soon as the ball was over (Julie felt committed to this undertaking), and she was sure of a replacement, she was leaving Bigelow Manor forever. She'd had enough of Mrs. Fynn's nastiness, Brad's cold indifference, Dan's sarcasm, Sophie's superiority, and Amy's open hostility.

She'd had enough readily explained accidents. And she couldn't help feeling alone although she realized a lot of it was her own doing. Jim was spending more and more time with Sophie, since Brad was spending more and more time with Amy. A reconciliation between the latter two seemed inevitable. Despite Dan's attempt to patch things up with Julie, he was with Sophie whenever Jim wasn't. Frank Palmer walked around with a haunted look, and Julie prayed that Brad would never find out why.

Julie kept telling herself she should be

glad to get away from the place, and she kept thinking about the note. Any one of them could have sent it to her. Still, Amy did seem the most likely suspect, since it had arrived the day after she did. And Amy made no bones about wanting Julie out.

I'd rather quit than give her the satisfaction of firing me once she's firmly entrenched here again, Julie thought. She promised herself she'd tell Brad of her decision the day after the ball.

"A penny for your thoughts." Mrs. Bigelow was looking at Julie quizzically.

Julie lifted her eyes from the list she'd been staring at unseeingly for the last several minutes and gave a self-conscious smile. "You shouldn't ask a girl a question like that the day before the grand ball."

Mrs. Bigelow, back to her chirpy-bird self, cocked her head to one side. "And don't I remember the excitement! What days those were. That reminds me, I promised you a ball gown, and I want to help you pick it out. Come along." She whirled up the stairs as if she were a young girl.

Julie trudged along behind. It seemed

the hundredth time she'd made the trip that day. Up one, two, three flights of stairs, through the double doors, and into a beehive of activity. Scaffolding was up, and the ballroom walls and the crystal chandeliers were being cleaned. The band was rehearsing on a small stage. Workmen were painting the railing on the balcony that opened off the rear of the big room. The wiring on overhead fans was being checked.

Mrs. Bigelow threaded her way through the bustling activity, chirruping encouragement to one and all. She had won the hearts of the workers already, and they responded with waves and grins. Her enthusiasm was infectious, and even Julie found that she felt more cheerful.

"Chester was going to have an elevator installed," Mrs. B. said. "Wouldn't that have been grand?" Brad refused to do it after Chester died. An unnecessary expense, he called it. I really don't understand how Chester and I could have produced such a boy. Why, he's even been fussing about the cost of this tiny affair."

Julie looked around at the swarm of

bodies all preparing for "this tiny affair" and smiled to herself. And as for Brad's fussing about the cost, the only thing he'd said was, "Don't make so much work for yourself, Mother. Keep it simple."

"Ah, here we are, dear." Mrs. B. flicked a light switch and opened the doors to the stuffy attic area in one of the turrets.

The large space was crammed with old furniture, bric-a-brac, and clothing. It made a rather interesting display, one Julie would have liked to examine more closely, but Mrs. B. had other plans for today. She walked to one side and whisked several dust sheets off a long rack nestled next to a wooden rocking horse. Julie imagined it might have been ridden by Brad when he was a youngster. Her eyes turned back to the long rack. A row of gowns covered with see-through plastic garment bags hung there most temptingly.

"A better selection than you'd find in any shop," Mrs. B. said proudly. "And believe it or not, I was as small as you when I wore most of these."

Julie felt like a child who couldn't make a selection from a huge tray of delectable pastries. The gowns were all exquisite and obviously very expensive.

Mrs. Bigelow, seeing her indecision, came to her rescue. "This is the one I had in mind for you," she said, opening one of the zippered bags.

She pulled out a lovely gown of pale-pink taffeta. It was so simple—so beautifully, deceptively simple—that Julie knew it must have cost a fortune even way-back-when. And the cut was so fine, it would make her look like a princess.

"Do you like it?" Mrs. Bigelow was becoming impatient with a star-struck Julie.

"No, I don't like it. I love it," Julie said softly. "I can't wait to try it on."

"Let's take it along then," Mrs. Bigelow said. "I have a dear little tiara downstairs that I wore with it. I can't wait to see you all done up. You'll be the belle of the ball."

Back down the stairs they went, stopping this time at the second floor. Mrs. Bigelow went along to Julie's room, calling Molly to come up in case any alterations were needed.

Julie changed in the bathroom. When

she made her entrance, her audience of two clapped their hands in appreciation. Molly pinned the areas that needed work, a tuck at the waist, a seam let out slightly in the bodice.

"You sure will be a hit tomorrow, Miss Julie," Molly said. "No one will be able to hold a candle to you." Carefully she carried out the lovely gown.

Mrs. Bigelow lingered for a bit, talking about the old days, talk that Julie always enjoyed.

When the old woman left for her own suite, Julie's spirits sagged once more.

After all, what good was looking gorgeous at a ball when there was no one special just for you? And how could you feel good in a house where you weren't wanted?

CHAPTER TWENTY

The day of the ball was cool and cloudy. Everyone was working feverishly on last-minute preparations for the big event. Julie was rushing around trying to get answers to all of Mrs. B.'s questions, for she had insisted her patient rest. Upstairs and downstairs she ran, an ever-present pad and pencil with her.

"Don't be checking up on me," Mrs. Fynn sputtered when Julie asked her about some decorations. "You take care of your own job and I'll take care of mine. I got along fine before you were here, and I'll get along fine after you're gone."

"Why do you say that?" Julie was immediately suspicious.

What made Mrs. Fynn think she was going away? Had the housekeeper written the note telling her to leave? Julie thought she had made some inroads in her relationship with this woman. They weren't exactly friends, but they treated each other with a certain distant respect. Now it looked as though their association had deteriorated to its previous level.

"Nurses come and nurses go," was Mrs. Fynn's cryptic answer, but at least she didn't have the bite in her voice that she once did.

Julie walked away, feeling a little better. There was much to admire about this mother of Dan's. She worked very hard, kept the entire house in meticulous condition, and cared a great deal about her son and his education. Occasionally Julie would look in her gray eyes and think she saw a twinkle very much like Dan's.

Next Julie looked for Sophie. For some reason, Mrs. B. needed to know the color of her gown.

"She says she and Mr. Dan are gonna be in the exercise room," Molly offered when Julie questioned her about Sophie's whereabouts.

Julie checked and, sure enough, there was Sophie riding one of the exercise bikes. She could have been a model posing for an ad. Dan was lifting weights, while his eyes roved admiringly over the neat form in the shorts and T-shirt pedaling effortlessly away. He remained completely unabashed by Julie's presence, giving her a big grin and a wink.

Julie grinned back, but approached Sophie in a more formal manner. "Excuse me, Miss Palmer," she began, "can you tell me what color gown you'll be wearing tonight? Mrs. Bigelow wants to know."

"I'll do better than that, kiddo. I'll show it to you," Sophie said, dismounting.

Having never had more than a polite, distant relationship with the doctor's daughter, Julie was too stunned by Sophie's sudden friendliness to say anything.

Sophie, ignoring Julie's lack of response, gave Dan her cool cheek to peck, told him she'd see him around, and strode briskly from the room. Julie scurried after her.

Then Sophie said, "Daisy wants to know the color of my gown because she's going to order flowers for me. And when they arrive, Brad's name will be on the card. Isn't that romantic?" She sighed. "Surely you've noticed how she's pushed the two of us together. Her biggest dream is a Palmer-Bigelow merger."

"And how about you, Miss Palmer? How do you feel?"

"I like Brad well enough," the blonde said carelessly. "And I wouldn't want to see Amy get her hooks into him again." She turned toward Julie. "And all along I thought you were the only competition."

"Me? How could you? I mean, I only work here. I hardly know the man."

"I had my reasons. For one, Brad must still have had feelings for Amy to hire you who look so much like her. Then, once I was around you, I found out you were different from that witch. You managed to combine the good parts of Amy, mainly her looks, with a—well, a pretty nice personality. What I'm trying to say is that you've got the good parts of Amy and not the bad. I also felt you were competition because Daisy was worried about you and—"

"I think you're wrong," Julie broke in.

"Mrs. Bigelow never indicated in any way that she thought anything like that."

"I've been wrong before," Sophie said. "So tell me, Miss Jacobs, which of our other two eligible bachelors do you plan to lay claim to tonight? Mr. Razzle-Dazzle Dan or True-Blue Jim?"

Julie stiffened. "I don't plan to lay claim to either," she retorted coldly. "So if it's an open field you want, Miss Palmer—"

"Tut-tut. Watch that temper. You've got me all wrong. What I want is a favor."

"A favor?" Julie couldn't imagine what she could do for this girl who had almost everything.

"Yes, a favor. Father has been acting so peculiar lately." So she's noticed, thought Julie. "I never thought he cared one way or another whether Brad and I made a match. But ever since Amy arrived, he's been edgy and upset. Maybe he cared more than I thought. I've never seen him like this except—except..." She drifted off, clearly absorbed in her own troubled thoughts.

"Except when?" Julie prompted.

"Well, he was here at Bigelow Manor at the time Amy disappeared, and he was very upset by the whole thing. Who wouldn't be upset with a police investigation and talk of murder and all? Afterward, Father flew off to Europe for several weeks. When he finally came home, he was more like his old self. Perhaps seeing Amy again brought those ugly scenes back. But why they should bother him so, I can't understand. Or else he feels the same as Mrs. Bigelow about Brad and me, and the reconciliation attempt is bothering him. I just don't know."

The beautiful face began to crumple, and soon tear streaks marred its perfection. For the first time Julie realized that under that veneer of cool sophistication was a young girl who suffered, worried, and loved exactly like everyone else. Julie moved toward her, but the blonde had recovered.

"I'll get the gown," Sophie said, for they had reached her room.

"What's the favor?" Julie asked when the other girl returned carrying a

spaghetti-strapped black gown with a
series of ruffles at the bottom.

"If you're not going to be tied up with
one guy, I thought maybe you'd pay a little attention to Father. Talk to him.
Maybe dance with him. He has me so
worried, and I can't seem to do anything
with him or for him." Sophie appeared so
distressed, Julie's heart went out to her.

"Of course, I will," she said kindly,
"and your gown is beautiful. It's something only you could do justice to."

"Thanks," Sophie said, drawing back
into her room. She popped her head out.
"For everything," she added with a warm
smile.

Julie thought about her encounter
with Sophie as she walked along the
hall. Dad had been right when he'd said,
"People are people no matter what their
station in life." She'd been brought up
with that axiom, but it hadn't been until
today that she'd learned it was true.
Ever since coming to Bigelow Manor, she
had felt inferior. At least her great adventure, which was rapidly coming to a
close, hadn't been entirely useless, she
told herself.

She passed Jim, who had been downtown picking up the tux he had rented. He was whistling tunelessly as he shyly held up his finery for her inspection. It was his first tux ever, for suits were as dressed up as people got back home.

"You'll be the slickest of the city slickers," she kidded him and watched his face light up. "I have to give Mrs. B. some messages now." She held the pad up. "But see ya later, Alligator."

His old high-school retort, "In a while, Crocodile," made Julie smile.

Then she stopped in her own room and reported her findings to Mrs. B. by intercom.

"How does the ballroom look, dear?"

"I'm going up to check now," Julie replied.

The ballroom looked magnificent. The walls were festooned with garlands of flowers, and handsome arrangements of more flowers surrounded the stage. A canopy was up over a long table with a champagne fountain in its center. Dainty gilt tables and chairs were arranged attractively. Dance programs were ready for the ladies, each made by hand by

Sarah and Molly since there was no time for printing. Ferns and other greenery were placed around the doors leading to the balcony.

Julie stepped through those doors. The newly painted wooden railings around the balcony also had garlands wound around them. The railings looked dainty and festive—and very frail. She absently began to check all of them to make sure they were in good condition and sufficiently sturdy.

Glancing at the back lawn, Julie found herself thinking again about Sophie. Obviously the glamorous blonde didn't know about her father's relationship with Amy. No wonder the poor girl was confused. She really was much nicer than Julie had ever imagined.

Funny, Sophie didn't seem upset by the possibility of losing Brad. Unless... unless... An ugly thought popped into Julie's mind. What if Sophie really had thought Julie was a threat? She could have written the note, and now when it seemed that Amy was winning Brad back, she might want to divert suspicion away from herself. What better way than to pretend indifference?

Oh, it doesn't matter anyhow, Julie told herself. I just have tonight to get through, and then everyone will know I'm going.

She walked back through the ballroom and downstairs wishing with all her heart she was a young, carefree girl going to her first ball with her Prince Charming instead of this worried, cynical unwanted inhabitant of Bigelow Manor, who had to leave shortly.

There was much activity on the second floor. Amy was calling out for a hairdresser. Maids were rushing around carrying garments, flowers, and other items. Everyone was excited except Julie, who entered her room with a heavy heart.

Then she saw the memo tacked to the cork board by the intercom. FROM THE DESK OF BRAD BIGELOW, it announced in large print across the top. The message was handwritten: "Meet me on the balcony at intermission. I have something to tell you—Brad."

Julie's spirits lifted.

CHAPTER TWENTY-ONE

"A fairy princess. That's what you are, Miss Julie, a fairy princess." Molly was pinning Mrs. Bigelow's tiara in Julie's dark hair, which fell in a cascade of curls down her back.

Princess. That was what Dan was always calling her.

"You're the one who worked the magic with this dress, Molly, making it fit perfectly. And without your help I could never have gotten this tiara to stay in my hair. If I'm a fairy princess, then you must be the fairy godmother."

Julie stared at her imagine in the mirror and suddenly thought of a mother, not a godmother, but the real mother who years ago had pinned a tiara on her head...

* * *

"Mommy, do I truly look like a princess?" Julie whirled her tiny five-year-old body around in its pink tutu, waving her magic wand in a way that made her tiara wobble precariously.

"Oh, yes, you do, sweetheart. But you must always remember that 'pretty is as pretty does.'"

"I'll remember. That means you must always be nice or you're really not pretty at all. Right, Mommy?"

"That's right, sweetheart."

"And if you're nice, everyone will always be nice to you. Right, Mommy?"

Her mother smiled. "Well, usually," she said, "but you can't count on that. You can only control your own actions."

Molly was preparing to leave. "It be a pleasure to do things for you, miss, but now I gotta run along because Mrs. Brad needs me."

Mrs. Brad! How quickly Amy had reinstated herself. "What color is she wearing, Molly?"

"Red. Bright red, and it looks ever so lovely with her dark hair. Still, she won't

hold a candle to you, I'm thinkin'. Funny,
I used to think you two looked just alike,
and now I can't see it. You're as different
as can be. Well, I better hurry along.
Have a good time, Miss Julie."

"I will." Julie took another look at
herself in the mirror and smiled approv-
ingly. She had never felt so beautiful
since that dance recital long, long ago.

She thought about Sophie's words:
"You've got the good parts of Amy and
not the bad." Could Sophie have been
right? Could Brad have been interested
in her even for a short time?

The thought was enough to make Julie
giddy. What did he want to tell her tonight? Perhaps Amy had already decided
to fire her and he had to break the news.
No, he'd never tell her that at the ball.
That would be too cruel.

Well, she'd just have to wait to find out
what he wanted.

With a pirouette, reminiscent of her
childhood ones, Julie dashed out the door
and up the corridor to the huge staircase.
Tonight white-uniformed attendants
were stationed at each landing to assist
and direct guests. The attendant on the

second floor smiled at Julie, and she smiled back.

Then she hesitated, not wanting to arrive at her first ball alone. Should she go back and see if Jim was ready? He was probably as uncertain as she was, she thought. Just at that moment, Jim and Dan emerged together from the guest corridor.

"Wow," Jim said, "you look terrific."

"Just like a real princess," Dan said, kneeling down before her.

"You may rise," Julie said regally. She looked them up and down. "Hey, you guys don't look half bad yourselves."

They grinned at her. The sound of doors opening and closing, and a soft murmur of voices preceded the appearance of Frank Palmer and Sophie around the bend.

"Sophie!" Julie used her first name without thinking. "You look even better in that gown than I imagined you would."

Sophie held up a slim wrist sporting a large white orchid corsage. "From Brad," she said, winking at Julie with a "told you so" look. "The gown better look good.

It set Father back a buck or two. What
do you two gentlemen think?" she asked,
leaning languidly against the bannister,
one hand on her hip.

Jim was impressed. "You look like—
like..." He was at a loss for words. But
then he came up with his highest acco-
lade: "Like Marilyn Monroe. Doesn't she,
Dan?"

"She's a knockout, all right," Dan answered, eyeing the cool beauty. "But I
think she's more the Grace Kelly type.
We have the pleasure of the company of
Grace Kelly and Shirley Temple." He
playfully pulled Julie's hair.

Sophie linked arms with her father,
who had remained silent during the ex-
change, and they all walked up to the
ballroom.

Brad, handsomer than ever in his tux-
edo, was greeting guests at the door, his
mother, resplendent in pale-turquoise
chiffon, by his side. He openly admired
Sophie's appearance and recovered
quickly from his confusion when she solemnly thanked him for the corsage.

Julie managed to suppress her amuse-
ment and thought she saw his eyes light

up for a moment as he shook her hand. But then he was politely turning to Frank Palmer, and she was passed on to Mrs. B.'s warm embrace. A sharp stab of disappointment struck her at the brevity of her encounter with Brad. In that moment, Julie knew without a doubt that she'd fallen in love with him—a man who scarcely knew she existed, a man who was in the process of making up with his estranged wife. She couldn't help looking forward to their talk on the balcony.

At least I'll have his undivided attention for one last time before I leave, she told herself, trying to relinquish the memory of his gentle touch and the softness of his voice as he'd called her "poor little girl."

I am a poor little girl, she told herself. A poor, silly little girl.

Julie was introduced to several of Brad's associates, including Homer Shaw, and their wives. But though she smiled and nodded, she was simply waiting for the intermission.

Amy was everywhere, vivacious in her red taffeta, as at home with the guests as with the family. No one would guess she'd been back only a week, for she gave the appearance of being the hostess of the evening.

And soon everyone will forget Amy's been away, Julie told herself, shaking hands with Walt Shandrew, described by Frank Palmer as Brad's personal attorney.

The band, or orchestra, as Mrs. B. preferred to call it, was good. Julie danced with Dr. Palmer, Mr. Shandrew, Jim, and Dan. She even had one dance with Brad, who had been charming on the dance floor with his mother, Amy, and Sophie, but who remained coolly aloof with her, an employer doing his duty, making no mention of their planned talk on the balcony.

"See you later?" Julie asked as he relinquished her to Dr. Palmer.

"Of course, Miss Jacobs," he said, looking slightly startled, before moving off to be claimed once again by his lady in red.

At last the musicians laid down their instruments and made their way to the canopied area, where every kind of treat imaginable was being served.

Julie, seeing Brad's head bobbing her way above the others in the sudden crush, edged toward the balcony, relieved that he had remembered. When she reached the double doors, she slipped through and walked over to the railing.

The breeze felt cool on her hot cheeks. And as her eyes grew accustomed to the darkness, she saw the balcony was being deserted as everyone prepared to eat.

Had Brad planned it that way? Julie was walking around the perimeter, enjoying the serenity, when she heard a sound on the lawn below. She was leaning over the railing, searching with her eyes, when someone pushed her so hard, the air escaped from her lungs in a little squeak.

Then she heard the sickening sound of splintering wood as the railing gave way.

CHAPTER TWENTY-TWO

Julie screamed as she felt the railing give way beneath her. She began to fall, and then something abruptly stopped her. It was the stout cord used for the flower garlands, still wrapped around her piece of railing, that was preventing her from dropping to the earth. Yet even if she could manage to hang on, which was becoming more difficult with every passing second, that cord couldn't support her for long.

When she screamed again, Brad's face peered down at her, and she saw him fumbling with the cord. She screamed louder.

Brad had lured her out here, pushed her over, and was now going to finish the job.

"Stop," she cried helplessly. "Stop!"

"Hang on. We'll get you." That was Jim's voice.

Julie felt a surge of relief. Hands were holding on to her wrists and pulling her upward. She heard the material of her gown tearing and felt the pain as her chin, then her chest, hit the edge of the balcony. Hands reached under her armpits, hauling her in like a big fish. She lay on the balcony gasping.

"You're safe now," Brad said. "That railing must have had dry rot. I can't believe those workmen painted right over it without noticing."

Jim was holding her head. "You're okay now, Julie girl. You're okay."

She could see Dan standing in front of the doorway.

"Everything's fine, but the balcony's a little weak. Better stay off it," Dan warned some people.

Apparently most of the guests were unaware that Julie Jacobs had almost been murdered. The thought of her near death sent a spasm of uncontrollable shaking through her body.

Brad slipped off his jacket and bent down to cover her, but she cried, "Get away from me!"

"Brad saved your life, Julie," Jim told

her soothingly. "She's so upset she doesn't know what she's saying," he added apologetically to Brad.

"I do, I do," Julie sobbed. "You don't understand. I was out on the balcony earlier. It was okay. Don't you see what that means?"

"There, there, you're safe now." Jim's words were meant to be calming, but she only became more distraught.

"He's trying to kill me!"

Brad turned to Jim. "She's getting hysterical. We've got to get her out of here, somewhere quiet, away from all these people. Mother's long evening cloak is hanging in the coatroom. It's turquoise and gold. Do you think you could get it? I'll stay here. No one will question you. But if I go in, they'll be all over me."

Julie was filled with terror. "No! No! Don't leave me here with him."

She clung to Jim, but he disengaged himself and stood up.

"Julie, honey," Jim said reassuringly, "I know how frightened you are, but you're safe now. Your boss here risked his life to save you. I saw it with my own eyes. Trust me. You know I'd never let anything happen to you if there was anything I could do to prevent it. Now I'm going to get something to cover you, and then I'm going to take you out of here. Please try to be brave just a little longer." He walked away.

Julie knew that what Jim had said about protecting her was true. She also knew that he didn't understand the present situation at all or he'd never leave her alone with Brad. She gauged the distance between herself and Dan, then wrapped her cord-torn hands around a piece of broken railing. If Brad made one move toward her, she would hit him with it and yell for Dan.

Brad did not make a move toward Julie. Instead he asked, "What were you doing out here all alone, Miss Jacobs?"

"As if you didn't know."

"Were you planning to meet someone?"

"You know I was."

"Who were you supposed to meet?"

"Come now, Mr. Bigelow. Don't play games. You know darn well who I was meeting."

"This may come as a surprise to you,

Miss Jacobs, but if I knew these things you keep saying I know, I wouldn't be wasting my time trying to find them out from a stubborn, hysterical woman. Now suppose you answer me."

Julie was furious. Her shaking was now due to anger, not fright. "You monster!" she shouted, pulling herself up and waving the piece of railing at him. "You send me a note asking me to meet you here, then try to kill me by pushing me through the railing. When, purely by luck, I'm saved by this flower garland, you try to pull that off. Jim's arrival stopped that attempt, so now you've gotten rid of him. And you have the audacity to try and make me believe—Oh, I don't know how I could have ever thought I was in..." Somehow she stopped herself before she said "love."

"You really believe I did all that?" Brad asked after a long pause.

"And there wasn't any dry rot," she continued in a steadier voice, "so don't try that excuse again. I was up here earlier, and every bit of this railing was firm. And see the ends of this." She waved the piece of railing again. "Smoothly cut, so you better get rid of

this bit of evidence if you're going to
make your innocent story stick. I don't
know why you want to be rid of me, but
I'm quitting. I planned to tell you tomorrow. So there was no need to...to..."
She couldn't finish.

At that moment Jim returned with the
cloak, which completely covered her. Unbelievably the tiara, though cocked at a
precarious angle, had not been lost.
Molly had anchored it very firmly indeed. Jim straightened it, and then, with
an arm around Julie for support, led her
to the balcony door.

She peeped through the glass. Couple
after couple whirled by, for the band was
now playing a lively polka. She saw a
very white-faced Mrs. Bigelow staring in
the direction of the balcony. Poor thing,
Julie thought, she's worried, and that's
not good for her blood pressure.

Julie wondered how she was to get
through all those dancers to the doors
that led downstairs. Dan took care of
that.

"Allow me," he said to Jim, transfer-
ring her weight to himself. "We're going
to dance out of here, princess."

"Of course," Julie said bitterly, placing

her arms around his neck. "Royalty must never make a scene."

"I have to meet with Amy and Walt Shandrew, my lawyer," Brad said, "but I'd really like to see that note, Miss Jacobs. You see, I never wrote it."

With torn hands, a ripped gown, and assorted cuts and bruises concealed beneath the long cloak, Julie allowed her weak legs to give up as Dan whirled her away.

The theatrical Dan never missed a beat. The way he was dipping and twirling, no one guessed that he was carrying the girl in his arms.

CHAPTER TWENTY-THREE

"I've brought you some tea, dear," Mrs. Bigelow said. "I've been so worried about you."

Julie sat up in bed. Her arms felt as though they'd been stretched on her mom's curtain stretchers, and her hands, wrapped in layers of white gauze, were as clumsy as boxing gloves. Her body did what she told it to, but not without letting her know that it didn't like it. Even smiling caused the abrasion on her chin to smart, and breathing did the same for her chest.

Two little paws and a white face appeared over the edge of the bed.

"Pekos," Julie said, smiling anyhow.

Satisfied that he was welcome, the miniscule canine leaped onto the bed as his mistress trundled a dainty tea cart across the carpet.

159

Mrs. B. said, "I know you're going to scold me and say you're the nurse, and you're supposed to be taking care of me, and I shouldn't be waiting on you. But I've done some reading, too, young lady, and I've learned that old people need to be needed, and that they're healthier in the long run when they can feel useful. You can't deny that, can you?" She stopped for breath and peered at Julie, her blue eyes gleaming with self-satisfaction.

Julie tried to look stern but was unable to suppress the laughter welling up in her chest. "I love you," she said, "but you're an old humbug. You never read that at all. You saw it on the soaps. Granny Fox told her nurse almost the same thing two weeks ago when Ginny broke her leg at the ski lodge, and they were snowed in and couldn't get help."

Mrs. B. feigned innocence. "Did she? I must have missed that one. Perhaps the writer read the same article I did." She was completely unconvincing, however, for she couldn't suppress her own laughter. "Anyhow, it does my heart good to see you smiling, Julie. They wouldn't let

me see you last night. They said you
were hysterical, and Dr. Palmer had to
give you a sedative. I hold myself respon-
sible. This wouldn't have happened to
you if I hadn't had that old ball. Let's
have some tea, and you can tell me what
happened."

She pulled up two white wicker chairs
and, while Julie clumsily slipped on her
robe, poured the steaming liquid and un-
covered a tray of toast and muffins.

Julie told her story, taking care to
keep her voice unemotional and to make
no accusations. After all, Brad was Mrs.
B.'s son. Julie ended with his denial that
he wrote the memo.

"Where is it? Maybe I could tell who
wrote it."

"That's the funny thing. Brad said he
wanted to see it, too, but it's gone—disappeared. I think the person who wrote
it retrieved it." She paused. "But there
are some people who think there never
was a note, that I made up the whole
thing. No wonder I got hysterical!"

The old woman's blue eyes were
thoughtful. "I believe you, and I think
you're right. The person who wrote the

note removed it. That's the only way it makes sense. After all, that would be evidence. It also occurs to me that we ought to get that piece of railing. That's evidence that may disappear too."

Mrs. Bigelow was probably right. There was no way Julie was going back to that balcony, however. But she skirted the issue for the moment. "So you do believe it was intentional?"

"I can see no other explanation, none that makes any sense. Can you, dear?"

"But who dislikes me enough to attempt murder? That doesn't make sense either."

"Dislike? I don't necessarily think they'd have to dislike you. More likely you represent some kind of a threat to them, or stand in the way of something they very much want."

"Who could I possibly be a threat to? I'm a nobody from the sticks without money, power, or influence. Besides, I've always tried to be nice to people."

"Being nice is no guarantee that the world will be nice to you, my dear. Besides, you're a very attractive nobody, which can sometimes be quite dangerous. Yes, you could have been viewed as a threat by a lot of people."

"Who?" Julie demanded.

"Well, let's see. There's Mrs. Fynn for instance. You must admit she's a sinister type, and she'd like very much to put a claim on the Bigelow estate. Apparently with spying and prying, she's found some old codicil that says that if Brad has no heir by the time he's forty—and that's only five more years—a portion of the estate is to be divided among all the single male Bigelows of his generation."

"That would include Dan," Julie said in a shocked voice.

"Yes. In fact, he's the only other single male Bigelow that we know of. If either Dan or Brad seemed attracted to you, Mrs. Fynn would find you a threat. By the same token, if Dan thought Brad might marry you, he could also view you as a threat."

"Dan? I won't believe it. Dan is as down to earth as—as Jim. He's got a temper, but he wouldn't hurt me. I know he wouldn't. Besides, what about Amy and Sophie? Nothing's happened to them. And if what you're saying is true, they'd have the same potential of ruining the chance of that codicil being worth anything."

"Not really. Sophie has often said that she doesn't want children, though I think she might be persuaded by the right man. And Amy is sterile. Besides, something did happen to Amy. She disappeared for several months."

"But wasn't that by choice? Didn't she hope to marry Dr. Palmer?"

Mrs. B. was startled. "I didn't know you knew that."

"But she did, didn't she?"

"Yes, she did. And even though it didn't work out, Frank loves her very much. If he thought you were standing between her and what she obviously wants, which is Brad—or for that matter, if he thought you were standing between Sophie and Brad—he might want to get rid of you."

"Not mild-mannered Dr. Palmer. Besides, he'd choose another way, a medical way." Julie thought of the blood-pressure pills and got goose bumps.

"Anyone can be aroused to violence if their emotions are involved strongly enough," Mrs. B. said sadly. "Sophie or Amy could want to be rid of you if they loved Jim, Dan, or Brad and thought you had the inside track. And, of course..." She stopped. "Now I'm getting you all upset, and you're not drinking your tea. And I feel all useless again." The blue eyes twinkled. "So drink up if you care about me, little one."

Julie lifted her cup as best she could with her bandaged hands and took a sip. Setting it back down, she put more sugar into it. "You haven't drunk yours either," she said.

"I've been too busy talking and scaring you half to death. Don't listen to a silly old person like me. I sometimes ramble on. I do think we should go get that railing, though."

"I don't want to go out on that balcony ever again," Julie said stubbornly. "Just look what happened to me the last time." She indicated her bandaged hands and multiple bruises.

"Of course, dear. But maybe after you've had a bit of your breakfast, you'll feel better and things will look a little brighter." Mrs. B. lightly patted her cheek. "Tell me, can you think of anyone who you thought might have pushed you last night?"

"I thought it was Brad," Julie said dully although she'd planned to remain silent on that point. "But he had no motive. It makes no sense at all."

"Sometimes murder doesn't make any sense." Mrs. Bigelow settled back into her new role of mystery unraveler.

Wonder what soap opera she heard that on? Julie thought affectionately.

"For instance, the person might be deranged," Mrs. B. went on. "Now Brad was a very strange little boy. Sweet and kind one minute, cold and indifferent the next."

Julie couldn't help thinking he hadn't changed very much in that respect.

"Sometimes he would turn violent, breaking toys and raging for no apparent reason. I thought he outgrew it, but apparently he didn't. I believe it was his viciousness which made Amy turn to Frank Palmer."

Julie doubted that. Of the two she suspected that Amy was the more vicious.

Then she reminded herself that Mrs. B. was letting her imagination run rampant.

"I wonder if he could be suffering from some malady, something that gives him these mood swings. Maybe it was Brad, Julie. Maybe he went out of control last night." Her voice had become melodramatic.

Julie sipped her tea, not knowing what to say. She was getting too sleepy to think straight.

"You know, my dear, I do remember him going by my room carrying a piece of paper yesterday right after I'd sent you to check the ballroom or something. He could have taken it and tacked it on your bulletin board. And remember how quickly he arrived on the scene after your fall in the wine cellar? He must have been the one to push you then, too. And he could have switched your medicine and put that other note in your book."

Julie's eyes grew heavy as Mrs. B. became more and more excited by her own conclusions. Still, she listened as closely as she could, feeling something was wrong with what Mrs. B. was saying. What was it?

"We better get that railing before Brad destroys it." Mrs. Bigelow was pulling at Julie, almost dragging her across the room.

"No, Mrs. B." Julie's words were slurred. "It wasn't Brad."

The last cog fell into place. She slumped to the floor. But before slipping into unconsciousness, she tried to read those blue eyes, for she knew she'd never told anyone about the note in her book.

CHAPTER TWENTY-FOUR

"Poor little girl. My poor little girl."

The words were far away, as though they were filtering down to Julie through a thick layer of cotton enveloping her head. It must be another weird dream, she thought, trying to wake up, but her eyelids refused to obey.

A fear tugged at her, something about her tea. Only, her memory couldn't or wouldn't dredge it up. She lifted a hand to try and push the fuzziness away, but it was impossible.

Am I dead? she wondered. Maybe I'm dying. Was there something in that tea? Maybe I'm dying from poisoned tea. I should try and tell someone, so they could help me.

Julie concentrated on her mouth and throat, but no sound came out though she could feel her lips moving.

"What is it? Are you trying to tell me something?" The voice was close now. It wasn't a dream.

Julie managed a drunken nod.

"Keep trying to talk. I won't leave you. When you're able to speak, I'll be right here."

It sounded like Brad. Wasn't he her murderer? That was long ago.

Julie stopped thinking and used all her energy to croak one word. "Poison."

"Not poison. A little too much sedation, but you'll be okay once it wears off."

She felt herself being cradled in two strong arms. Soon she felt nothing at all.

When Julie next woke up, a hand gently touched her shoulder. It was Brad's hand.

"Hi," he said. "How do you feel?"

"The way I imagine a person with a hangover must feel. Awful." Julie tried to grin. "Oh, Brad!" She suddenly remembered. "Where's your mother?"

"She's in her suite. Molly's watching her, and she'll let me know at once if—if anything comes up." Julie searched his face. "Yes, I know," he said gently, "at least part of it. I'm afraid I suspected,

but I couldn't believe it. I was coming to
see you this morning hoping I was
wrong, but when I arrived, Mother was
just leaving, and you were on the floor.
She said she was going for help—to find
Dr. Palmer. I lost my head and forced a
different story out of her."

"Why did she do it, Brad? I don't understand."

"It's a story that began a very long
time ago. My dad spoiled her outrageously, giving in to her every whim and
throwing his money away foolishly in an
effort to keep his Daisy happy. She was
so beautiful then, and he thought he
would lose her if he opposed her in any
way. Therefore, her every wish became
his command. By the time of his death,
he had squandered most of his assets. If I
had any heirs, he wanted the mansion
and his remaining assets to go to them.
But if not, he wanted his estate shared
with single Bigelows. That was his way
of saying that a guy who wasn't worried
about keeping a wife happy might handle money a little more wisely. It was a
strange will, and the codicil wasn't discovered until recently. Apparently he

had contacted Mrs. Fynn and told her about it, and that's actually why she came here. Anyway, when I talked to Shandrew last night, he said the whole thing wasn't legal. There weren't even any witnesses. I went ahead and made provisions for Dan's future with my lawyer. Because with a lot of luck and a few good investments, I've been able to restore the family fortunes to a modest extent."

"I can see why Mrs. Fynn was so awful to me at first. She was afraid I was getting too attached to Dan and might ruin his chances at some money. But I still don't see why your mom would... would..."

Brad sighed. "No matter how well I do, it's never enough for Mother, who dreams of returning to the grandiose days of the past. When I married Amy, I extinguished all hopes she had of my marrying money. The marriage was a mistake right from the start for more important reasons. I shouldn't call it a mistake. I should call it a disaster. As it turned out, Amy was also only interested in money. They say men often try to marry someone like their mother. Well, in that one way, I guess I did." Brad looked sheepish for a minute. "The lure of greener pastures beckoned to Amy, and she had hopes of marrying Frank Palmer, a truly wealthy man."

"You knew that?"

"Of course I did. I've tried to keep it quiet, since I thought it was best for all concerned. But there were rumors which caused the police to investigate, and I had to tell them the whole story. After that, the divorce went through with no hitches. There were just too many witnesses who knew the truth."

"You're divorced?" Julie said.

"Of course."

"But you told me the portrait in the library was of your wife."

"The divorce hadn't been finalized at that time."

"But I thought you and Amy were reconciling. You told me last night that the two of you were meeting with your lawyer."

"We did, but that was only to make sure everything was understood on both sides. Amy may have had some different ideas when she came back, but there was never any chance of a reconciliation."

"There's something else I really have to ask you."

"What might that be?"

"Why did you ask for a picture in that want ad? Why did you hire me, someone who looked so much like Amy?"

"I'm coming to that. After Amy was gone, Mother was lonely and wanted a companion. I thought it would be good for her, but I was determined never to get involved with a woman again. To protect myself, I asked for a photo, planning to hire the most unattractive nurse I could find." He grinned at Julie.

"And that was me?" she asked, unable to disguise the hurt she felt.

"When I saw your photo and the resemblance to Amy, I was shocked. Then I told myself that you would remind me of that money-hungry, witchy female every day. What better way for me to keep free of female entanglements? So I hired you —and promptly fell in love with you."

"You did?" There was no hurt in Julie's voice now.

"It was the worst thing I could have

done. Though I fooled myself for a time, I couldn't fool Mother. She wasn't going to allow me another penniless bride. She imported Sophie and did everything she could to keep you away from me."

"Including hitting me over the head in the park?"

"No, Julie. That's what threw me off the track. I knew Mother had nothing to do with that, for I was with her at the time. If it wasn't an accident, then I thought it had something to do with Dan and his mother. But I was able to discount that theory because Mrs. Fynn was also here, and Dan didn't know about the codicil at that time."

"Then who did it?"

"No one. I'm convinced that was your one bona fide accident. It's what gave Mother the idea that an accident could be arranged, and it's what made me believe the other things must be accidents, too."

"Then Mrs. Bigelow did switch the pills?"

"It was easy for her. She got you to go along to her own room, poured the blood-pressure pills while you lay there with a cloth over your eyes, waited till your medication arrived, and in all the confusion left the wrong pills handy and the right ones hidden."

"Did she think they'd kill me?"

"I think she was just hoping you'd be frightened and want to go back home."

"And she pushed me in the wine cellar?"

"Actually, she just slammed the door shut, which knocked you down. Another attempt to frighten you off. When she heard me coming, she stepped into the cooler. And then when I went down to get the champagne, she slipped back to the game room, where we found her dancing."

"I know about the notes," Julie said. "That's how I knew she had to be involved. Both times she knew exactly where I'd be so that she'd have free access to my room. She couldn't have damaged the balcony railing, though, could she?"

"It didn't seem possible, but that fancy work got its strength from its structure, not its size. The spindles and railings were very small. She used the small saw from the hobby set in the game room. If you hadn't been so upset last night, thinking I'd done all sorts of murderous acts, you'd have found it in the huge pocket of the cloak, just as I did this morning. That's what sent me hurrying to find you."

Julie remembered those railings, and how they'd looked so fragile that she'd tested them.

"But how did she know I'd stand in just the right spot?"

"She lured you there by throwing a champagne glass. I found the remnants of it on the walk today. You heard it break when it hit, walked over to investigate, and she pushed you. She immediately slipped back inside. In fact, she was already inside, though near the door, when I ran out."

"Why did she dope me today? I thought it was poison."

"To finish the job. You were supposed to go out on the balcony to get the railing, but you'd be groggy from the tea laced with Dr. Palmer's sedatives, and easy to push over."

Julie shuddered. "She was always such

a dear. From the moment I met her, I was drawn to her. I—I really loved her, and I thought she was fond of me, too."

"She was, Julie, she was. She just wasn't used to someone standing in the way of what she wanted."

Julie started. That was what Mrs. B. had been trying to tell her this morning. She had been so sad as she explained that murder might have nothing to do with dislike. Julie thought of all the good times, the giggling, the camaraderie, the caring, and she knew in her heart that that was the real Mrs. B. All the rest was merely a symptom of a serious illness.

"What's going to happen to her?" she asked softly.

Brad bowed his head. "I'm not sure," he answered heavily. "I suppose she'll be put in an institution."

"Oh, Mr. Brad!" A white-faced Molly ran into the room, tears rolling down her cheeks. "I think Mrs. Bigelow is dead."

Brad started to his feet, but Molly wouldn't stop talking.

"I stayed with her like you said. Honest I did, Mr. Brad. She was just sittin' there drinkin' tea, cup after cup of tea.

'You gonna be fit to bust,' I told her. 'Help me lay down,' she said. 'I want to rest.'

"Then she was sleepin', and I sat there readin', some moving magazines all this time. I noticed it got extra quiet and I gave her a look. And it was like she wasn't breathin' no more. I touched her and she didn't pay me no mind."

A new torrent of tears cascaded down her cheeks. "Oh, Mr. Brad," she wailed. "I think she up and died on me."

Julie tried to get up from her bed to go to her patient.

Gently Brad restrained her.

"Let it be, Julie. Let it be." He turned to the weeping Molly. "There, there," he comforted her, a haunting sadness in his face and voice. "Maybe it's for the best. We didn't realize it, but Mother has been sick for a very long time."

CHAPTER TWENTY-FIVE

The blue-and-yellow-plaid valises were packed and neatly stationed near the door. Julie glanced around the pretty room that had become her sanctuary at Bigelow Manor.

It was funny, she thought. The room was exactly the same as it had been upon her arrival. Yet she was so changed.

You did a lot of growing up in this room, Julie girl, she told herself.

A look in the dressing-table mirror assured her that she was still Julie Jacobs, but it also revealed a subtle change. She had a softer, more mature look, the look of a young woman who knew who she was and where she was going.

A soft knock on the door told her that it was time to leave. The door opened.

"Ready, hon?" Jim stood waiting there,

180

his shy smile lighting up the earnest brown eyes behind his glasses.

She nodded, grabbing her purse as he hoisted the luggage. She followed him down the stairs to the entry hall, where the Tiffany lamp still glowed dimly and the velvet chairs still flanked the ornate mirror.

Molly was there, this time without her feather duster. The tears, which had seemed almost continuous since the death of Mrs. Bigelow, were coursing once more down her round red cheeks.

"I sure will be missin' you, Miss Julie," she sniffled as she wound her arms around Julie and gave her a wet squeeze. "And so will this little guy," she said, pointing to Pekos, who danced around Julie's feet, not looking sad at all.

Mrs. Fynn handed her a basket. "I had cook prepare you a bite to eat in case you get hungry on the trip," she said in her reserved manner.

"Why thank you, Mrs. Fynn," Julie said and surprised herself by kissing a cool cheek.

Mrs. Fynn blinked and then, her manner softening just a trifle, said, "I told you nurses come and nurses go, but I didn't think you'd be going so soon. It won't seem the same around here without your flighty ways."

Dan gave Julie a crushing bear hug. "I don't care what anyone says," he whispered. "You'll always be a princess to me."

The Palmers and Amy had taken their leave right after the funeral, so there was only one other person to say good-bye to.

"Guess I better go collect my last paycheck," Julie said casually as they all stood watching her, their expressions inscrutable.

She knocked at the door to Brad's study, then gently pushed it inward.

"Well, hello, Miss Jacobs," he said. "What can I do for you?"

"I came to collect my paycheck," she said solemnly, "and to say good-bye."

He reached down and picked up an envelope lying on his desk. "I added a little bonus. I hope you'll find it to your liking," he said, "for your service here was very satisfactory."

"I'm sure I will. Thank you, sir."

He came around the desk. "Do you mind if I walk you to the car?" he asked.

"Not at all. That would be very nice, sir."

They fell into step, making their way through the little group that followed at a discreet distance.

At the edge of the driveway, they stopped and turned to look at the mansion. Julie couldn't help remembering the first time she'd seen it and how frightening it had looked with the dark clouds surrounding it. This morning the sky was brilliant.

She squeezed Brad's hand. "No shadows over Bigelow Manor today," she said.

"Miss Jacobs," he said, twisting the new diamond on her left hand, "it won't be sunny for me until you're back here in September as Mrs. Brad Bigelow." He swept her up in his arms and kissed her as if he'd never let her go. "Then," he said firmly, "there'll be no more shadows ever."

"The time will pass quickly," she promised, "and you'll be coming to Norson every weekend." She knew he hadn't wanted her to leave at all, but she had to. She had to be married in her own town, in her own church, in Doreen's gown made by her own mother.

Besides, engaged girls from her home-town didn't stay in the same house as their fiances before the wedding.

"It just isn't the done thing," she'd told him. And that was that.

Julie now looked across the lawn and saw, not the dear people assembled there, smiling at them, but the children of the future, running and playing: a handsome Brad Jr., a rough-and-tumble Chester, who would be a favorite of Uncle Dan and Aunt Sophie, and a beautiful little blue-eyed Daisy, who would be taught very carefully that the best things in life couldn't be bought by money.

Before the scene faded away completely, Pekos suddenly burst from Molly's arms and ran across the lawn delightedly, as if he, too, saw the future children and couldn't wait to join them.

978-0-595-45359-7
0-595-45359-7

Printed in the United States
92321LV00002B/469-498/A